# *All the Way to Wits' End*

# *All the Way to Wits' End*

*Sheila Greenwald*

*An Atlantic Monthly Press Book*
LITTLE, BROWN AND COMPANY
BOSTON TORONTO

*Second Printing*

*Library of Congress Cataloging in Publication Data*

Greenwald, Sheila.
All the way to wits' end.

"An Atlantic Monthly Press book."
SUMMARY: Eleven-year-old Drucilla longs to rid herself of her dusty, traditional family heritage but finds the price of conformity more than she wants to pay.
[1. Identity—Fiction. 2. Moving, Household—Fiction] I. Title.
PZ7.G852Al [Fic] 79-15936
ISBN 0-316-32670-4

ATLANTIC–LITTLE, BROWN BOOKS
ARE PUBLISHED BY
LITTLE, BROWN AND COMPANY
IN ASSOCIATION WITH
THE ATLANTIC MONTHLY PRESS

MV

Designed by D. Christine Benders

*Published simultaneously in Canada*
*by Little, Brown & Company (Canada) Limited*

PRINTED IN THE UNITED STATES OF AMERICA

To Sam and Ben Green

*All the Way to Wits' End*

# Chapter ONE

Drucilla Brattles stood in the middle of her new living room and knew she had been right. This was an awful house.

"If you make up your mind that it will work out here," her mother was saying from the depths of a carton across the room, "it will." Mrs. Brattles drew her face up. Her cheeks were flushed pink and her hair was every which way. "Moving days are always bad, Drucilla. Now for heaven's sake, cheer up."

"I didn't say anything," said Drucilla.

"You don't have to. You look like a thundercloud. Come help me unpack these things. It will take your mind off being homesick."

"Homesick?" Drucilla mumbled. "I thought *this* was home."

"You know what I mean," Mrs. Brattles said. Then she lowered her voice and stepped toward her daughter. "Look, Drucilla, I'm depending upon you. Esmeralda and Courtney will be watching you. If they see you hating this house, they'll hate it too. You have a strong influence on them. Please show them that you really like it here."

"Like it?" Drucilla's eyes widened. She looked at the cartons waiting to be unpacked, the chaos of packing paper mounting like weird sculptures all around them, and the bare, unlived-in, dingy rooms. Like it? If she pretended to like it she would appear as crazy to her younger sister and brother as her mother did to her.

Mrs. Brattles put her hand on Drucilla's shoulder. "You are eleven years old," she said. "You've never given me any trouble. I'm asking you to try very hard to understand. We had no choice. We could not stay on at Coves Landing. We simply could not. There were all sorts of reasons. We had to move and now we have to make the best of the move. I'm asking you for your help."

"I'll help you unpack," Drucilla said.

"That isn't what I mean." Her mother frowned. "I mean, help me to help us get used to *this*." She gestured hopelessly at the room. "I know it's small and strange compared to what we had. But we were living in a fool's paradise. Your father couldn't find work at Coves Landing and he can here. We certainly didn't need a twenty-six-room mansion, for heaven's sake, even if it had been left to us by your grandparents. We couldn't afford to heat it or maintain it." She paused and when she spoke again her voice was softer. "It was wonderful to live in a place surrounded by cousins and uncles and aunts, but we'll have to learn to get along without the family too."

The mention of all their family living on happily at Coves Landing made Drucilla feel even worse. "Couldn't we have kept just one of the rooms?" she said, thinking of her own.

"Of course not. We were lucky to sell the house. Anyway, we've got all our cherished things." They both looked around them again. The house was crammed with the huge pieces of furniture Drucilla's parents had inherited along with the house at Coves Landing. Generations of Brattleses and Bundages had collected these treasures, never dreaming that they'd end up jammed into a six-room split-level in a subdivision called Pitney Place. Not only did the Brattleses have to contend with the furniture, but also with cartons full of china, silver, linen, and clothes. Yes, they certainly did have their cherished things, but where on earth, Drucilla wondered, would they put them? Though she had been raised not to express her opinions, Drucilla had plenty of them.

She had known in her bones that Pitney Place would be terrible. She leaned into a carton and drew out a plastic-wrapped portrait of her great-grandmother Emily Crawford Bundage. Carefully she undid the wrapping and gazed at the dim, placid eyes, short thin nose, and the mouth. The family called it the Bundage mouth. Drucilla knew it well. Her mother had it and so, heaven help her, did she. The Bundage mouth meant that you could not get your lips together unless you thought about it and pressed them shut by force. Back home at Coves Landing where there were so many of these mouths in the family, it may have been known as the Bundage mouth, but here at Pitney Place Drucilla suspected there would be other names for it. "Bugs Bunny," she said out loud to the portrait.

"What was that?" Mrs. Brattles looked up from the lamp she was assembling.

"Nothing."

"Now Drucilla, you did say something. It might do you good to start expressing some of your thoughts instead of holding everything in and looking so stormy."

"We are a funny-looking family," Drucilla said.

"What an odd thing to say."

"We are, though. We have funny old hand-me-down clothes and funny old hand-me-down furniture and funny old hand-me-down teeth."

"Drucilla, I don't know what you're talking about."

Apparently Mrs. Brattles's idea of Drucilla expressing her thoughts hadn't worked. Mrs. Brattles looked more upset than before. Drucilla wondered if some of the thoughts she had expressed had occurred to her mother as well. But the door bell rang, startling them both out of any thought at all.

"Oh dear, what now?" Mrs. Brattles said under her breath. Courtney and Esmeralda came running down the steps to see and they all rushed to the foyer. Mrs. Brattles opened the front door against a driving rain. A small light-haired woman in a yellow slicker teetered on the threshold, looking as if she might be enfolded by her huge umbrella.

"Hello," she said, "I'm your neighbor, Peggy Noland. We live at number twenty." She pointed to the house on the left, folded up the umbrella, and stepped neatly into the foyer.

Mrs. Brattles stared at her, unbelieving and disapproving.

"Moving days can be horrible. I don't want to bother you, just to say hello and welcome to Pitney

Place." She put out her hand; rain drops flew off her slickered arm.

Mrs. Brattles shook the offered hand stiffly. "I am Cordelia Brattles," she said in her primmest voice. "These are my children, Drucilla, Esmeralda, and Courtney."

"Drucilla, Esmeralda, and Courtney," Mrs. Noland repeated. "What unusual names."

Mrs. Brattles drew back, as if she were stepping away from this remark. "Drucilla is eleven, Esmeralda is nine, and Courtney is three."

Mrs. Noland looked pityingly from one to the other of them. "My girls are Toni and Geri and Didi."

Drucilla closed her eyes. She had been right again. Even their names were weird. Oh how she longed for any one of those wonderful names. Toni, Geri, Didi.

Her mother was saying, "Drucilla, Esmeralda, and Courtney have been names in our families for generations." Then she laughed the high squeaky laugh which meant she was nervous. "In our family we keep the names alive, the silver polished, and the crystal shining long after other people might think it makes any sense."

Mrs. Noland looked at the jam-packed rooms. "You've got plenty of all of them," she said, "and I know I'm holding you up. If it would help at all, please send your girls over to visit. They can just ring our bell."

"Oh we wouldn't impose." Mrs. Brattles grew flustered. "They would never do that without calling first. I wouldn't allow it."

"But it would be perfectly all right with me," Mrs. Noland assured her as she stepped back into the rain. "So suit yourself."

After she had closed the door, Mrs. Brattles leaned against it and pressed her hands to the side of her head. She looked to Drucilla as if she were about to buckle. "I didn't do that very well," she said. "I'm not awfully good with new people."

Silently Drucilla agreed. She now felt she would have to add to her list of peculiarities the fact that they not only looked peculiar but acted peculiar. For a moment Mrs. Brattles appeared as if she might actually weep. But then she stood up straight, clapped her hands together as if to dispel misery, and said, "Now then. I think what we could all use is a nice cup of tea."

"Tea?" Drucilla said. She was aware of Esmeralda and Courtney staring at her and so she stopped herself from saying, "What good would that do? Tea."

"Yes, we need the silver and the tea service. Now where would they be?"

Drucilla knew it would be useless to protest. Mrs. Brattles in the throes of one of her ideas was not to be resisted. She had a way of becoming enthusiastic that was famous in the family. Once she overcame her shyness she couldn't do anything halfway. Whether it was selling raffle tickets or running a bake sale or working as a part-time librarian, her enthusiasm swept everyone along. Sometimes it was very exciting, but it could be frightening as well.

Drucilla trooped after her mother, along with Courtney and Esmeralda, and watched as she flung stacks of sheets and tablecloths out of a carton in search of the proper blue linen cloth. A crumpled piece of newspaper, used to wrap a cup, lay at Drucilla's foot. She picked it up and smoothed it out. It showed an advertisement for carpeting. On what seemed to be miles of soft blue carpet sat a mother, a father, and three young children with a large brown dog. They were all smiling. They wore bright clean clothes. A fire burned in a fireplace on one side and behind them spread a comfortable, warm, and beautiful room. Drucilla closed her eyes. "If I could have a wish," she thought, "I would open my eyes and be the girl on the carpet who lived in that room on the soft blue carpet." She opened her eyes. Mrs. Brattles had just found the linen cloth.

Waiting for the water to boil, Drucilla sat down

by the kitchen window. She wiped a spot clear and gazed out the window at the rain, across the yard and into the eyes of a girl about her own age. The girl looked back through her own window and then she smiled. Smiling was the worst thing you could do with a Bundage mouth. So Drucilla nodded and turned away.

Mrs. Brattles was busy pouring out the boiling water when the telephone rang. It was their first telephone call, and like everything else in this new house it was perfectly awful.

Drucilla heard her mother greet her father and then groan into the mouthpiece. "Oh no, Winston. What terrible luck. I don't even know a sitter. Drucilla will have to manage, that's all. It's an emergency. I'll be there as soon as I can. Now where exactly are you?"

While her mother ran to fetch a pencil and piece of paper, Drucilla said to Esmeralda, "I guess I get to baby-sit you."

"I don't want you to," said Esmeralda. "I never let you do it before and I won't let you now, and neither will Courtney."

Courtney looked from one to the other of them. He nodded his head agreeing with Esmeralda, but at the same time seemed afraid to go against Drucilla.

"That's just too bad for both of you," Drucilla

snapped. "I don't think you get to choose and from now on, Courtney, speak for yourself. You have a mouth. Don't let Esme put words into it for you."

"You can baby-sit me," Courtney said readily.

"But not me," Esmeralda said, and turned her back to both of them.

"Hush," Mrs. Brattles motioned to them. "You get no choice, Esmeralda." Then into the telephone she said, "I've got it all down. I'll be there as soon as I can. Of course you must make that interview, but oh Winston," her voice wavered and to her horror Drucilla watched a single tear roll down her mother's cheek. "Very soon now, I shall be at my wits' end." Wiping the tear with the back of her hand, Mrs. Brattles replaced the receiver. "Daddy's car broke down. I've got to go and pick him up and take him to that interview. Drucilla, I expect you to keep things under control until my return. Don't open the door to anyone. Don't tamper with the stove or fiddle with the faucets." All the while she spoke she was buttoning herself into her raincoat, fastening its hood and assembling her various keys. Then she smiled in a brave pathetic way and took Drucilla's face in her hands. "Set an example . . . you know." With that, she flung open the door and was out in the howling, lashing, drenching day.

When they heard their mother's car pull out of the

drive, Drucilla looked at Esmeralda and Courtney on the opposite side of the table. Courtney began to cry. The house was even worse than before. Drear encased it. With their mother gone, the stacks of boxes and heaps of paper appeared menacing. The clutter of tea things upon the table was the only bearable sight. Drucilla wished that the very first time she got to be in charge wasn't at Pitney Place. Had they been home, really home at Coves Landing, she would have known exactly what to do. She would have organized a game of hide and seek that could have lasted for hours in the immense house. Or she would have taken Esmeralda and Courtney to the drafty game room and they would have played dominoes or billiards on the table that smelled of mildew and had had its baize felt chewed by mice. Or perhaps one of the aunts or cousins would have stopped by for a visit. They would be so impressed to find Drucilla in charge and doing such a good job. Drucilla would have taken them into the kitchen and rummaged around in the bread bin for some crackers and then made a party in the dining room where they could have looked at the rain through the colored diamond-shaped glass of the leaded window. The rain, her father's car breaking down, her baby-sitting would have been altogether lovely, if they had been home in Coves Landing.

Esmeralda began to whimper. Drucilla looked frantically around. What was she to do? Then her eye lit upon the pile of linen and blankets still scattered on the floor. "Stop crying," she ordered. "Stop this instant. We're going to take a journey."

"A journey?" Esmeralda stopped in amazement. "How can we, Drucilla? It's pouring rain and Mother said not to open the door."

"We won't open the door. But we will take a journey." Pulling herself together on the basis of their interest, she spoke in a strong commanding voice she imagined to be like that of Grandmother Brattles. "We are taking a journey in a large traveling vehicle all the way to . . ." She tried to think of a good place, other than Coves Landing. Then she remembered where her mother had said she was soon going to be. "All the way to Wits' End."

Esmeralda looked dubious. "When do we leave?"

"As soon as we've made the vehicle," Drucilla said. "Let's begin."

# Chapter TWO

"But it's got no steering wheel and no controls," Esmeralda whined, "How can we drive it?"

IT was the vehicle Drucilla had made out of sheets and blankets draped over a very large carton in the foyer.

"We'll have to make them." Drucilla began to look around. "Here," she cried, "is our steering wheel. One of Aunt Marianna Richard's little round tables that we used to have the telephone on." She tipped the table on its side and it was just as she had said, a steering wheel. Next, they drew dials and clocks with a pencil upon the torn-off cover flap of a packing crate. The vehicle when finished was large enough to fit two kitchen chairs for a front seat and two for the back. The windshield was made by stretching a piece of plastic wrap between the edges of the carton. They positioned two flat tennis balls for a brake and accelerator.

"Shouldn't we take food?" Esmeralda said.

"Yes, and something to cook it in." They fetched some pots and bowls from the kitchen.

"Cookies," Courtney at last made his contribution. He scooped up a box of soggy gingersnaps.

"Are we ready then?" Drucilla examined the outside of the vehicle. When it met with her satisfaction she bent down to enter. The others followed. She settled herself before the steering wheel. Esmeralda and Courtney took the back seats.

"Oh wait," Courtney wailed. "Oh I forgot the animals."

"Do we have to take all of them?" Esmeralda protested. "Can't we ever go anyplace without the animals?"

"No." Courtney was adamant.

Drucilla sighed. "Go get them."

Courtney bounded out of the vehicle and returned moments later with a tattered cloth bag, full to the top with the shaggiest, sorriest assortment of stuffed animals ever seen outside a museum. Of course they were old, and had been sucked on, bitten, and kissed by generations of Brattleses and Bundages. Courtney held the bag tightly to him.

"Are we really ready then?" said Drucilla.

"Ready," came the reply from the back seat.

"Ready, ready ready ready," Courtney said in a high squeaky voice for the animals.

Drucilla put her foot on the tennis ball that was the accelerator and pushed down. "We are going to Wits' End," she said. "But the trip is very, very DANGEROUS."

"You didn't tell me that," Courtney said.

"I thought I shouldn't frighten you," Drucilla said. "But we have to go over very difficult roads."

"Why?" said Courtney.

"Because it will be a better adventure," said Drucilla.

"Are there good roads without adventure?" said Esmeralda.

"No." Drucilla was getting angry. "Stop being stupid. The whole point is that we're going to have adventures."

"You didn't tell me that before," Courtney said again.

Drucilla slammed her foot on the tennis ball that was the brake. "I never should have taken you," she hollered. "You are being a baby and ruining the

trip. Now get out of the vehicle this instant if you're too frightened for adventure."

"I knew you wouldn't be a good baby-sitter," Esmeralda complained smugly.

Courtney nodded agreement and clutched the animals tighter.

Drucilla took her hands off the steering wheel. They were ganging up on her. She closed her eyes and wished that something amazing would happen.

Something amazing happened. There was a mighty crack of lightning and the vehicle was plunged in darkness.

They sat perfectly still. The only sound was of water dripping close around them. "I'm sorry I said that about your baby-sitting," Esmeralda whispered. "I don't like this adventure, Drucilla, I want to go home."

Very softly Drucilla said, "We really can't." For she knew that the whole house was dark. She heard Esmeralda begin to sniffle.

"I mean really home," Esmeralda sobbed. "To Coves Landing."

"Me too," Courtney said. In no time they were both crying.

"Be still," Drucilla said. "I hear something."

They all listened. There was the drip drip of water falling on the blanket stretched over their heads and then over that sound they heard a loud pounding on the front door.

# Chapter THREE

"We can't open it," Esmeralda said. "Mother said we must not open it. MUST NOT."

Drucilla eased herself slowly out of her seat and groping in the shadows pulled the blanket aside. She stepped from the vehicle. "I am in charge of this adventure," she told them. The room was not quite so dark as inside their vehicle. A gray light came in through the window in the front door. The door itself was shaking, for someone was pounding on it with great force.

It was not often that Drucilla disobeyed her mother. She told herself that opening the door was part of the journey to Wits' End. It was against her mother's orders, but this was a new house, she was the new sitter, and she was making some new rules. She opened the door. A blast of wind seemed to blow it nearly off its hinges. Mrs. Noland in her bright yellow slicker stood on the sill with her huge umbrella in one hand and a flashlight in the other.

"Heavens, you poor things," she gushed. "I thought I saw your mother drive off alone and I knew you were here all by yourselves with the power out. Why on earth didn't she bring you over to my place? Good Lord, what a mess." She beamed the flashlight into the foyer and stepped inside. "I wanted to tell your mother that this house has more leaks than a sieve and a roof like a blotter. The Crossmans who lived here before you practically drowned everytime it drizzled. Now what on earth have you been up to?" She flashed her light on the vehicle. "Good grief, look at that."

"We were taking a journey," said Drucilla.

"Of course you were. Anybody in his right mind would want to get out of here." Mrs. Noland reached out and parted the blankets and shined her light into the vehicle. "Hi there," she bellowed at Esmeralda and Courtney. Her eye fell upon Aunt Marianna Richard's telephone table. "Yea Gods, what's a beautiful piece like this doing in here?"

"It's our steering wheel," said Courtney.

"It's one of Aunt Marianna Richard's telephone tables," said Drucilla.

"One of?" Mrs. Noland exclaimed. "You mean to say there are more?"

"Three," said Drucilla.

"Three. My dear child, three of these tables would get you a new roof and a good secondhand car."

"It's just an old table," Drucilla protested.

"And I'm just an old antique dealer who happens to know what she's talking about," said Mrs. Noland. "But that can wait. I came to bring you to my house. Let's get Aunt Marianna's steering wheel out of the rain." She scooped the table up in one hand and Courtney in the other and deposited them both on a dry section of floor.

"We don't have our coats," said Esmeralda. "They're still packed."

"Then you take the umbrella and run like blazes for my front door." Handing the girls her umbrella she picked Courtney up again and tucked him under one arm as if he were a sack.

In the few minutes it took Drucilla to dart through the puddles and downpour that separated her new house from the Nolands', she realized they were breaking her mother's rules. They were visiting without calling first. They were intruding upon strangers. They were leaving their own house, and in doing so she knew they had probably broken another twenty rules she didn't even know about. But when Mrs. Noland opened her front door to a foyer and living room exactly like the Brattleses' only completely different, Drucilla forgot all the rules. Candlelight flickered on an orderly, cozy scene. There were no cartons, crates, and puddles. It was just like the carpet advertisement.

Seated on the sofa were two girls hunched over a Chinese checkers board. Three candles burned in a small candelabrum. "You see," Drucilla whispered to Esmeralda and Courtney, "the vehicle has taken us to the Castle of Soft Light." She hoped this description might ease their minds about breaking rules and redeem her status as a good sitter.

"Toni and Geri, meet your new neighbors," said Mrs. Noland. "Toni is eleven and Geri is ten," Mrs. Noland paused. "I can't for the life of me remember your names."

Before she even knew she had said it, Drucilla blurted, "I'm Gigi and this is my sister Coco. My brother is Courtney."

"Coco?" said Esmeralda in great surprise.

"Gigi and Coco?" Mrs. Noland looked confused. "I thought you were something else."

"We are," Drucilla said hastily, "But Gigi and Coco are what our friends call us."

"I'm Coco?" Esmeralda said, still quite bewildered.

"Of course you are," Drucilla informed her. She watched Esmeralda consider this with a shrug and funny smile. Drucilla felt herself grow light, as if her real name had been a weight upon her.

"Would you like to play fours?" said the sister named Toni.

"Sure," said Drucilla and she and Esmeralda sat down on the soft rug while Mrs. Noland took Courtney into the kitchen with her. "Come on, Courtney, Didi is eager to meet you," she said. At this point the lights came on. Geri and Toni blew out the candles while Drucilla and Esmeralda set the marbles upon the board and looked around them. The room was as soft as the rug, and the furniture was as wonderful and unreal to Drucilla's eye as the names Toni and Geri had been to her ear. Everything seemed to be pale and new and round. There were no deep shadows hiding rickety little tables on spindly legs. There were no carved uncomfortable chairs and lumpy sofas with the smell of ages in

them. There were no heavy old portraits in thick frames. Instead there were these soft white shapes all curved and delightful and solid to sit upon. Drucilla had never seen anything like it. She loved everything she saw. Toni and Geri looked vivid and bright, like the happy girls in the carpet ad. When Toni smiled, she showed a mouth full of wired teeth. Her sister's eyeglasses were framed in green with beautiful sparkles of red and gold. It was as if the braces and glasses were clever ornaments to make the perfect picture seem more real. Drucilla looked from one to the other, then down at her smocked dress with its drooping collar. It had been bought for Aunt Lucinda Bundage twenty years before, and it had been worn by at least three cousins in turn since then. Every time it was passed along somebody in the family would say, "See, when you buy quality how it lasts and lasts." It was true it had lasted, Drucilla thought. It was also true that Aunt Lucinda had been plump and Drucilla was skinny and that the neck and sleeves gaped. Drucilla knew that she looked awful.

In the middle of the game of Chinese checkers Mrs. Noland brought in a tray of hot cocoa and biscuits. Courtney was in Didi's room showing her his animals. Just then Mrs. Noland called, "Your mother is back. Her car is pulling in. I'll go tell her where you are and ask her to let you stay for the rest of the day."

The rest of the day? Guiltily Drucilla wished that they would never have to go back to wet and gloomy number twenty-two, that she might remain, become a Noland child and stay for good.

When Mrs. Brattles came late in the afternoon to pick them up, she stood in the Nolands' kitchen with her shoulders straight and her face shiny. "Time to come home," she said happily. "I have set up your rooms and put the kitchen in order and cooked dinner. Daddy got a lift. He's on his way home. He has some important news."

"Did you leave our vehicle?" Drucilla asked.

"Of course I did," Mrs. Brattles laughed. "It may be the only one in the family before long."

Mrs. Noland raised her eyebrows and sucked in her cheeks and looked as if she were trying not to say something. Then she stopped trying. "This is none of my business," she said. "I'm very poor at beating about the bush. I saw a simply fantastic table in your house. The children said there were more like it." She paused dramatically. "My dear Mrs. Brattles, as an experienced dealer in antiques, I can assure you that should you ever wish to part with one of those tables you could get a nice vehicle of your own. Two of them would bring you a brand-new roof."

Cordelia Brattles's face clouded with bewilderment. "We have many fine old pieces, Mrs. Noland, that is true."

"Oh call me Peggy. I know, I know your family collected them for years and years and I'm shocking you with my crass suggestions. But that house of yours needs a lot of fixing. Sometimes painful decisions and choices need to be made."

"Thank you for taking the children, Mrs. Noland. I am extremely grateful to you for your kindness." Drucilla heard her mother's voice climb an octave and knew how upset she was by what Mrs. Noland had just said. "You are kind also to take our problems so seriously and try to offer advice. I realize that you mean well."

"It isn't only that," Peggy Noland was warmed by Mrs. Brattles's response and eager to talk more. "It's that I'm a practical person. We've had our ups and downs too. I suppose most people have. I know about painful choices from my own experience. Believe me, braces cost a lot of money, and glasses too. Roofers and plumbers can be a fortune, but they make our day-to-day lives a lot easier. A Chippendale table can be an enormous luxury."

"I don't know what you're talking about," Mrs. Brattles said in her highest, thinnest voice.

Mrs. Noland seemed to realize that she had gone too far. "Forgive me," she said. "I am an awful butinsky. I've done it again. But that is a beautiful piece of furniture; keep it out of the rain."

Mrs. Brattles put out her hand. "Again, thank you for taking the children," she said stiffly and then ushered Drucilla, Esmeralda, and Courtney out of the Nolands' house.

It was clear to Drucilla that unpacking had made no difference at all. The large old dark wood pieces of furniture stood around like lost victims of a museum fire. The rooms were shrunken and sad. The most cheerful place to be was in the vehicle.

Just as she thought this, Drucilla heard her father's key in the latch. The door opened into the gloomy foyer. Mr. Brattles was so overjoyed that the room itself magically changed around him. "Everybody," he called. "Come hear this." In the family they said that Mr. Brattles got his hopes up too much and was too trusting and could never understand why things didn't work out. But Drucilla loved the way he got enthusiastic. When he was happy his red hair seemed redder and a pink light came off his kind ruddy face. When he was happy he seemed actually to glow. Tonight for the first time in months he was glowing. He waited until they had all assembled and then, beaming upon them, said, "I got it. I got the job. The one I wanted." For a miraculous moment the house at Pitney Place seemed warm and happy.

However, the next morning, after breakfast, Drucilla found herself looking at the telephone table of Aunt Marianna Richard's with resentment. She remembered Mrs. Noland's words. "If we sold that old thing we could get a new car," she thought. Then she had a startling idea. If we sold all these old things we could be like the family in the carpet ad, sitting there on miles of soft floor, a fireplace in the background and lovely things all around. She pictured braces on her teeth and new clothes too, and not looking like a creep. She pictured sitting on the carpet in a bright dress with her teeth wired straight and smiling at people. The people would be smiling back and they would be classmates from her new school. The school she would be starting in just one week. Suddenly she felt desperate. She realized she would be starting that school in one of Aunt Lucinda's dresses, and with a Bundage mouth. She walked to the kitchen door.

"Where are you going?" Mrs. Brattles said.

"I have to go to the Nolands' to find out something important," Drucilla called as she stepped out the back door.

"Don't impose, Drucilla, please," Mrs. Brattles's voice followed her outside. As she hurried across the small patch of lawn on that bright cool morning, Drucilla felt a burst of tingling spirit surge through her. She was in a new place and felt all sorts of possibilities within herself to be a new person. Exactly who that person was she wasn't quite sure. Her feelings changed so quickly since they had been at Pitney Place that it made her giddy. She had made decisions, been a baby-sitter, met new people, and now felt the beginning of a vague but shocking new idea. The rain had left the sidewalks and paths clean. The grass was deep and still wet. There was a feeling of fall in the air. Drucilla saw Mrs. Noland with Toni and Geri out back in their garage. They were busy doing something and didn't notice her till she was standing next to them.

"Hello there," Mrs. Noland boomed. "How's life today?"

"Terrible," said Drucilla happily.

Mrs. Noland put down a cracked lamp she had been holding. "We're up to our necks in this garage sale."

"Garage sale?" Drucilla was confused. "Are you selling your garage?"

Geri and Toni hooted and Mrs. Noland laughed. "A garage sale is when you take all the old junk you've accumulated and have no use for and set it out in your garage or your lawn or driveway and try to sell it to some lucky customer. We run garage sales a lot around here, don't we girls? I'm a big junk collector. You'd be surprised how often my junk is somebody else's treasure."

Drucilla remembered what she had come to find out. "How much exactly is our table worth?" she said.

Mrs. Noland blinked in surprise. "I couldn't tell you exactly. I would have to look it up in my catalogues."

"What catalogues?"

"The antique dealers' catalogues where prices are listed."

"Could I see your catalogues please?" said Drucilla in a hushed voice.

"Why, of course," said Mrs. Noland. Then with an expression that was both quizzical and amused she went into the house to fetch them.

Drucilla watched Geri put a little tag around the

leg of a very tattered teddy bear. In Magic Marker she wrote "95¢."

"Ninety-five cents?" Drucilla was amazed. "Will you get that much?"

Geri grinned. "I'll never know unless I try to find out," she said. "Like this old vanity set." She pulled open a box full of pink plastic bottles, a mirror and compact. "I never used it. I think it's dumb. I bet it brings in a dollar. Then I can get something I really want."

"Like what?"

Geri looked vague. "I'm not sure," she said. "I've opened a bank account from the last garage sale. I cleared about five dollars that time. So I might just add to it and let my interest grow."

Mrs. Noland had returned with a stack of catalogues and magazines. "I don't have the time to go over these with you now, Gigi," she said. "You'll have to go through them yourself. But I'm sure you'll find your table somewhere."

"I'll return them as soon as I can," said Drucilla gratefully. She saw her own mother standing on their kitchen doorstep, waving to her.

"Drucilla," Mrs. Brattles called, "I need you to take Courtney and Esmeralda for a ride in that thing so that I can unpack." She nodded stiffly to Mrs. Noland. "I hope my daughter isn't imposing."

"Heavens no," said Mrs. Noland. "Gigi is always welcome."

"Gigi?" said Mrs. Brattles confusedly.

"Please, why don't you all come over later when our sale is on."

"We'll see," said Mrs. Brattles coolly. She held the door for Drucilla. "Who is Gigi?"

"Gigi?" Drucilla said. "Oh, Gigi." She drew out the name to give herself time. "Gigi is what my friends call me," she said, as if "didn't you know?" "They call Esmeralda Coco."

"Gigi and Coco? Oh my goodness." Mrs. Brattles rubbed her chin. "I don't know if I can get used to that. It sounds so strange. And what are those magazines for, Drucilla?"

"I don't know," Drucilla answered truthfully. She didn't know just yet, but something, some exciting idea had certainly begun to root in her mind.

# Chapter FOUR

It wasn't till Courtney went in for his nap at two-thirty that Drucilla and Esmeralda were able to go over to the Nolands' garage sale.

"Did you sell the teddy bear?" Drucilla called to Geri.

"Yes, I got my full price," Geri hollered back. "This is the best sale we ever ran, even though it's a weekday. Mommy sold the busted toaster oven, the bagel slicer and the toilet paper roll cover."

"And that hideous sweater set from Aunt Josie," Toni added.

"Oh it was fantastic," Geri said. "I love a garage sale."

"We have lots of stuff left, though," Mrs. Noland said. She was checking over the objects remaining on the table.

"How much stuff did you sell and how much did you make?" said Drucilla, pulling a pencil and notepad out of her pocket.

"Let me think a minute," Mrs. Noland looked over at Drucilla. "What on earth are you doing, Gigi? Taking notes?"

"I'm getting some information," said Drucilla, her pencil poised over the pad.

"Information on MY garage sale?"

"It seems the best way."

"Best way to what?" Mrs. Noland said. "I am bewildered."

"To go about my plan," said Drucilla. "Would you please answer a few questions?"

"Yes, of course." Mrs. Noland pulled her face into a more serious expression. She answered all of Drucilla's questions and waited as she wrote down the answers. How many objects had been sold? How much money had been made? What sort of objects did best?

Just as she was finishing up with her notes, Drucilla saw a car pull up. A group of women and children spilled out.

"Hi there, Eve Mallory," Mrs. Noland called.

One of the women waved hello and they all came up to view the goods. A skinny boy with straight long pale hair and two chipped front teeth stood by the side of the car.

"Chipper," Toni said to him, "this is Gigi. She's going to be in our class."

"Oh yeah?" He looked over at Drucilla and she could see his eyes go right to her front teeth. She glued her eyes to his, while trying to press her lips together.

"H'lo," she said.

"H'lo who?" he said.

"Chipper?"

"That's right. I'm Chipper. I know who you are. You're Bugs Bunny, right?" After he said this he grinned broadly and tapped his two front teeth.

Drucilla realized that he was trying to establish a bond between them, something they almost had in common. But she hated the bond. Having something the matter with the way you looked was no reason for friendship.

"What are you selling?" Chipper asked Toni. "Do you still have that fortune-teller's ball?"

"Gone," Toni said. "I told you you should put a reserve on it. A thing like that goes very fast."

"Very fast?" Chipper said. "You've had it through two garage sales and one tag sale."

Toni shrugged. "It was under things."

Chipper was distracted, going up and down the tables picking up this and that.

His mother had already collected an armful of small items. "Honestly Peggy, you have the cutest stuff," she said. "I just love this compote dish. Never saw one quite like it. But seventy-five cents?" She groaned. "A little high, y'know."

"I bet I see it at *your* garage sale next week for a buck five," Mrs. Noland said.

"Mmmmmm," Chipper's mother didn't answer.

"Hey Bugs," Chipper said to Drucilla. "Do you know which section you'll be in?"

"She's in our section," said Toni. "Mrs. Best."

He made a mock-threatening face at Drucilla. "Watch out, we're all mean in Mrs. Best's section."

"Oh stop it, Chipper," Toni said. "Go away." She turned to Drucilla. "He's the biggest tease in the school."

Right again, Drucilla thought. Now her worries about starting at the new school were no longer vague. They had a face and a name . . . Chipper Mallory.

After the Mallorys left, Mrs. Noland decided to take down the signs. "I'm through," she said. "These sales are fun, but they tire me out. I've got to begin dinner anyway." She started toward the house and then remembered something. "Gigi, I hope you don't take Chipper Mallory seriously."

"He didn't wait a minute to call me Bugs Bunny."

Toni shook her head. "I don't understand why you don't get braces like me," she said.

"Don't ask nosy questions like *me,"* said Mrs. Noland, and she went into the house.

"My two front teeth stuck out like a shelf," Toni said happily. "But in only three months of these wires, I could close my mouth. Dr. Gregory said I would, but I didn't believe him. He has comics in his waiting room." They were putting all Toni's unsold stock back into a large basket. Esmeralda was helping Geri carry her goods back to the house.

"We could never afford braces," said Drucilla

slowly. "We have to be very careful about how we spend our money. My father was out of work for a long time and we have debts. My parents say, No Extras. Braces are extras." She paused and decided to let Toni in on something. She drew closer. "I have a plan though. Maybe it will change things."

"What?" Toni lowered her voice to a whisper. "What's your plan?"

"Why do you think I'm taking notes?" Drucilla held up her notebook.

"A tag sale?" Toni caught on. "Listen," she hissed. "My mom says there's a gold mine of antiques in your house, if you'd sell them." Then she burst out laughing. "My mother says, your mother would die first."

"We'll see about that," said Drucilla. "Some information may change her mind."

"Do you really think so?" said Toni.

"I won't know unless I try," Drucilla said uncertainly.

As she walked back to her house she rehearsed what she would do. She felt that she had enough material to make her presentation. She spent the rest of the afternoon poring over the catalogues and jotting down figures. She knew that she needed to have her arguments perfectly clear and solid. She knew that if her scheme were to work she would need to convince her parents with every shred of information she could find. That was how Drucilla was. Orderly and organized. She made lists, took careful notes, and planned and plotted. Back at Coves Landing it had been her reputation (along with never giving any trouble). "That child could run an organization," her grandmother had once said. Drucilla didn't want to run an organization, but she did want to run her own life a little.

And so at dinnertime when Mr. Brattles asked, "And what did you do today, Drucilla?" she was ready.

"I went to a wonderful garage sale at the Nolands'."

"What was so wonderful about it?"

"My friend Toni made five dollars and Mrs. Noland cleared over fifty."

"Cleared over fifty?" Mrs. Brattles scoffed. "Drucilla, what a funny way to put it."

"It's not funny," Drucilla said. "They cleared over fifty by selling stuff they didn't need and couldn't use."

Mrs. Brattles's face clouded. "I don't understand how people can do that sort of thing. Don't their belongings have any meaning for them? How can they put them on the selling block? I could never think of such a thing. It would be like selling parts of myself."

There was silence for a moment as Mrs. Brattles passed the beans around and then, clearing her throat, Drucilla said, "I don't agree."

"What do you mean?" asked her father.

"I mean that I looked up Aunt Marianna Richard's table in the antique catalogue and I'll bet if we sold it I could have braces and some new clothes." She reached under her chair for the catalogue. "If we sold a few of our things we could get a new roof too." She was aware of speaking too fast and of Esmeralda staring at her dumbstruck, with cheeks full.

"What has come over you, Drucilla?" her mother

said in alarm. "Please try to remember who you are. You are not someone called Gigi. You are Drucilla Brattles, who used to know how to behave appropriately."

"Somebody called me Bugs Bunny," said Drucilla. "I want braces. I hate my teeth."

Mrs. Brattles shook her head in disbelief. "Your teeth," she said. "You have the Bundage mouth. I know that sometimes it isn't easy to have the Bundage mouth. I, of all people, am aware of that. But Drucilla darling, you must accept who you are and love and respect yourself and not be ashamed. Your teeth are *you,* Drucilla. They are part of the wonderful person you are."

"Not anymore," said Drucilla.

"Not Drucilla Brattles anymore?" said Mr. Brattles, bewildered. Then gently he said, "Only the place has changed, Drucilla. Only the house where we live. We are the same people. We just moved, that's all."

"Only the house where we live," Drucilla said, "and the school where I'll go and look like a creep and be called a creep and it isn't the Bundage mouth, it's MY mouth and I hate it. I'll hate it for years and years, till I'm fifteen and never smiled."

"Control yourself, Drucilla," said her mother, "remember who you are."

"I don't know who I am," Drucilla said and she picked up the catalogues and magazines and fled the table.

She sat down in the vehicle out in the damp foyer. She stared at Aunt Marianna Richard's telephone table and for a dizzy moment she really didn't know who she was. She had once been Drucilla Brattles of Coves Landing, organized, well mannered, never-gives-any-trouble. Now she desperately wanted to be Drucilla Brattles of Pitney Place. But her parents wouldn't allow it and so she was no one at all. She was stuck.

# Chapter FIVE

On the first day of school Drucilla found out that she had been right again. The minute she saw Chipper Mallory and two other boys sitting at the first table in the lunchroom opening paper bags of food, watching her, she felt it in her bones: TROUBLE. Sure enough, Chipper nudged the boy next to him, Brucie Phelps, and pointing to Drucilla said, "Bugs Bunny," and stuck out his own two chipped teeth in imitation of her mouth. Drucilla bent her head and kept walking. Their voices followed her.

"Bugs is very very shy," Chipper said loudly.

"So would you be if you had her other name. Her real name," Brucie said.

"What other name?"

"She's not Gigi. I saw her real name in the attendance book. She's Droo Silly."

"Droo Silly?"

"Yeah—Droo Silly and Sillier."

Chipper roared. Then Brucie Phelps banged his feet, and this caused the other three boys at the table to laugh till they lost their breath.

"Gigi," Toni called to Drucilla over the din. "I'm saving you a seat over here."

Drucilla slipped into the seat. Toni introduced her to a pair of twins named Alice and Mary Lou who were eating on the other side of the table.

"Don't listen to Chipper," Mary Lou said. "He's stupid."

Stupid or not he and Brucie had ruined the first day. Drucilla had gone up to Mrs. Best, her teacher, before class began in the morning to tell her that Gigi was the name she always used and please not to call her Drucilla in class. Mrs. Best had smiled and said, "Yes, of course, dear." But all Drucilla's precautions had not worked out.

"Where do you get your funny clothes?" the twin named Mary Lou said, interrupting her thoughts.

"They were my mother's or my aunt's or my

cousins'," said Drucilla. A piece of sandwich stuck in her throat.

"I never saw any clothes like them," Alice said.

"I think they're so beautiful," Toni sighed over-enthusiastically. "They're like no other clothes, Gigi. You always look so different."

There it was. Weird clothes, terrible teeth, and peculiar name. Different. She had been right one hundred percent.

The following morning she was not surprised when she entered class to be greeted by ominous titters. On the blackboard she saw a caricature of her face and under it, in case anyone hadn't figured out who it was, her name: "Droo Silly."

Brucie was staring out the window, his neck splotched red and his hair spiky.

Mrs. Best came into the room, saw the blackboard and erased the picture. "That *is* silly," she said.

Later, as they were going into lunch, Toni hissed, "Gigi, don't let them bother you."

She said this because Drucilla was hesitating outside the door to the lunchroom trying to think of some way to get out of having to go inside. Chipper and Brucie were already at the first table waiting for her.

"When they see how much they can bother you,

they get worse," Toni said sensibly. "Laugh at them."

"I can't," Drucilla said. At the moment she could hardly talk.

"Well I can't wait out here with you," said Toni crossly. "I want to eat my lunch."

She started through the door.

Drucilla panicked. She could not risk losing her only friend. She followed Toni into the room.

"Beep beep, there she goes. Hey what's up, Doc?" A carrot stick was thrust under her nose and she was aware that her legs were not working very well. She followed Toni to the table where the twins already sat. There was another girl at the table. She was small and blonde and her name was Chrissy. She viewed Drucilla coldly over her carton of milk. "Why do you tell people you're Gigi," she said, "if your name is Drucilla?"

"It's a nickname," Toni answered for Drucilla. "Even though Drucilla is *such* a beautiful name. She thinks it's too long."

"It *is* too long," Chrissy said. "I don't know whoever said it was beautiful." She rolled her eyes.

Alice giggled. Alice seemed to be impressed by Chrissy. In fact both twins appeared to want to agree with every word Chrissy said.

"I never heard of such a name," Chrissy went on.

Obviously what Chrissy hadn't heard of was not worth hearing. "It's so *odd.*" Again the twins nodded in agreement. Drucilla tried not to look at Toni. If she found her nodding too, she would know she had lost completely.

"I still think it's beautiful," Toni said weakly. "And anyway, you can't do anything about the name your parents give you."

*"She* tried to," Chrissy said accusingly of Drucilla. "What do you think she pretended to be Gigi for? Gigi, yuch. It's stupider than Drucilla." With this verdict she closed her empty container and stood up. "I'm going to the yard. Come jump rope when you're done."

Being discussed by people as if she were not there made Drucilla feel as if she was in fact "not there." She assumed that Chrissy had not included her in the invitation, but she didn't know what to do with herself. She was embarrassed by her own presence.

The twins watched Chrissy go, then quickly finished their lunches so that they could follow her. They seemed embarrassed too, as if they could not wait to leave Drucilla's table. "Chrissy is so lucky," Alice said as she and her sister went out to join her.

Drucilla wondered why Chrissy was so lucky. Was it for her pale hair? Or her cold, confident manner? Or the way she had of telling you you had a stupid name and peculiar clothes? Toni was silent, and Drucilla guessed that she was longing to get up and join the others in the yard. If she did, Drucilla didn't know what she would do.

"Let's go out," Toni finally said, resolving the problem. "If we don't jump rope with them we can do something else." With Drucilla behind her, Toni walked up to Chrissy and the twins. "Can we join?"

"*You* can," Chrissy said. Then she looked pointedly at Drucilla. "I guess she can too."

When it was her turn to jump, Drucilla concentrated very hard. She was a good jumper, and she wanted to be at her best. She knew the game and didn't miss at the start. The singsong jingle buzzed about her ears. "Marco Polo went to France to teach the ladies how to dance." To her left she heard a jeering voice join her own, "To teach the Sillies how to dance."

"First a kick and then a bow," she went on, not losing her beat. "Marco Polo showed them how." But Brucie's voice was louder than hers. "First a kick," he hooted and then Drucilla felt the sting of his sneaker on her shin.

The rope stopped turning. Chrissy flung the wooden handles violently to the ground. She leaned forward, her pale face amazingly red, "Get out of here. Leave us alone," she screamed at Chipper and Brucie.

They ran off bleating in mock terror. Chrissy turned toward Toni. Her rage had receded with her color. "I knew this would happen if *she* played," she said icily, flicking her head toward Drucilla. Then she stormed back into the building.

It was time to go inside anyway. Another wonderful day at school.

Later, on the way home from school, Toni said, "Why do you let them do that to you, Drucilla? Why do you let Chipper and Brucie treat you that way? Why do you take that stuff from Chrissy?"

"What can I do about it?" Drucilla said hopelessly.

"Something." Toni was exasperated. "Think of something. I thought you had a plan."

"I did," Drucilla said. "But it didn't work." They walked for a while in silence.

"Want to come in for milk?" Toni said when they got to her house.

"No thanks." Drucilla could see that Toni was relieved.

Her own house was quiet. Esmeralda was at a friend's and Mrs. Brattles had gone to the library with Courtney. The vehicle loomed in the foyer. It had become Courtney's favorite place to sit. He had insisted that they not dismantle it. Drucilla and Esmeralda liked to get into it occasionally too. It

looked ridiculous and ramshackle to Drucilla. "Even our games are weird," she thought, stepping carefully around it to go upstairs to her room.

She flung her book bag down on her bed and then flung herself down beside it. Think of something? Make a plan? How could she. She was stuck. She gazed furiously at her bedside table. She detested it. It had a glass top under which was a wreath of flowers made of real human hair by her great Aunt Cora London. The human hair had belonged to second cousin Muffin Egli. On top of the table was the silver comb and brush set of Granny Crawford's with the teeth all out of the comb and the brush bristles soft as cat fur, useless. Even her things were creepy. Her things. Then it came to her. They were *her* things. They belonged to Drucilla Brattles of Pitney Place. She sat bolt upright on her bed. She had thought of something. She had a plan. She was going to get unstuck.

# Chapter SIX

Toni noticed the change in Drucilla. "You don't seem to mind the boys' teasing anymore," she said at lunch the next Monday. "What's up? Why did you ask Mrs. Best if you could do some special things in the art room after lunch?"

"You'll see," Drucilla said.

"See what?" Toni cried. "What are you going to do? I can't stand the suspense. You have to tell."

Drucilla folded her waxed-paper lunch bags into a little heap. "It's a project."

"What project?" Chrissy said. She had been sitting on the opposite side of the table toward the far end gazing out the window. Drucilla had no idea she was listening. "If you don't tell us soon we may all get tired of waiting."

"Then get tired of waiting," Drucilla muttered. The plan had given her courage to talk back, even if it was under her breath.

Chrissy pouted. "Doesn't your mother ever buy you anything new?"

"Underwear and socks," Drucilla said. The subject was a sore one.

"I happen to love that dress," Toni said. "Drucilla looks like a picture out of an old book."

"That Old Book Look," Chrissy dusted crumbs off her orange wash-and-wear slacks. "Looks good in old books." She got up to put her bags in the garbage. It was raining so there was to be no yard play.

Drucilla and Toni and the twins started for the door. As they passed Chipper's table Drucilla quickened her step.

"Catch any flies lately?" Chipper said.

Drucilla looked away. "I have to go to the art room," she said to Toni.

"What were you talking to Mrs. Best about?"

"She said I could use a sheet of oak tag for a poster."

"A poster for what? Come on, Drucilla—you've got to tell me."

Drucilla considered. She had already told Esmeralda, who had been so horrified that she said she didn't know if she could help at all. Of course the real secret had to be from her parents, at least till she got things set. Then they would surely know. What they would do about it would be anybody's guess. "Okay," Drucilla said. "I suppose you can help me out."

"How?" Toni gushed.

"You could keep the poster I'm going to make at your house until I'm ready to use it."

"Sure." Toni clapped her hands. "When will that be?"

"On Saturday, if it doesn't rain. My mother is working at the library that morning. My father likes to sleep late and I'm supposed to baby-sit Courtney and Coco."

"What is the poster for?"

Drucilla took a deep breath. "A tag sale," she said.

"But you told me your parents wouldn't allow it."

"A tag sale of MY OWN things," said Drucilla.

"Oh Gigi."

"Then when I make some money I'll call your Doctor Grant and get my teeth wired up just like yours."

"Oh Gigi," Toni wailed. "What will your mother say?"

"They're MY things," said Drucilla, not answering the question at all.

They entered the art room where Drucilla had set aside a piece of oak tag. In the fifteen minutes remaining of her lunch hour, she became completely engrossed in the lettering and designing of her poster. Toni watched and made comments over her shoulder.

"Don't you think it should have more colors?" Toni said.

"No." Drucilla was copying the words out of her notebook. "I want it black on mustard. Black on mustard really stands out." In fact she had planned out every small detail of this event. She was the old purposeful, organizing, list-making Drucilla. She kept a page of her notebook on which to write ideas for her tag sale. She loved to go over every detail. Where the poster would be placed, the selection and arrangement of the objects on the driveway, the apron with pockets that she would wear to put her change in, the little cash box, the tags for labeling. She had planned for everything. All that remained was the event itself.

On the Saturday morning of her sale, Drucilla awoke to a clear bright day. She thought this was a wonderful omen. Mrs. Brattles was having her breakfast of coffee and toast down in the kitchen. She was the only one of the family up. "Good morning, sweetie," she called gaily as Drucilla came in. "What a lovely day." Mrs. Brattles was all dressed in her suit and had her purse and gloves on the table. Ever since she had gotten the job at the library three mornings a week, she had been more cheerful than Drucilla had ever known her to be. For the tenth time she said, "I just love this job at the library. I can't believe my good luck to have gotten it." She chewed her toast thoughtfully. "Of course it wouldn't be possible for me to do it without your help, Drucilla. Don't think I'm not grateful to you. You've been wonderful to look after Courtney and Esmeralda so that Daddy can sleep. He needs his rest. He's got a bad cold." Drucilla noticed the eternal smudge of lipstick on her mother's front teeth. Bundage teeth always got lipstick on them. She fastened on this detail so as to drive away her nagging feelings of guilt.

"When I get home, I'll treat you all to lunch out at the Pancake House," Mrs. Brattles said. She pressed a napkin to her lips, put the empty cup in the sink, kissed Drucilla's forehead, and put on her gloves. Just before she let herself out the back door she turned to Drucilla. "People always said how lucky I was because you never gave me any trouble, Drucilla. It's more than that now: you've given me a hand."

As soon as her mother was out the door, Drucilla

tore up to her room. She got into her clothes and started to lug furniture and objects downstairs. She worked quietly so as not to wake anyone. She crossed off each job as she finished it on her notebook list. She didn't want Esmeralda and Courtney bothering her with their questions while she was setting up and so she let them sleep. She placed the pair of human-hair night tables and her découpage toy chest in the driveway. On top of them she arranged the comb and brush set and three silver-topped hairpin boxes. Then she carried the coat rack out of the foyer and from it she hung the dresses she most despised. Under the rack she arranged a pair of gremlin dolls inherited from cousin Gertrude Bundage. They had most of their stuffing out, were missing eyes, and had a bad smell. Then she sat down at the kitchen table with her envelope of tags and a felt-tipped pen and started to write prices. This was a problem. She had not been able to find the tables or clothes in the catalogues Mrs. Noland had loaned her. She couldn't gather information about them without giving away her plan. Therefore she had to make up prices which she hoped were reasonable. In the middle of this job Esmeralda came into the kitchen.

"Oh Drucie, you're going to do it," she said worriedly. "Oh, aren't you scared?"

"Be still," Drucilla snapped. "And listen while I tell you your job."

"My job?"

"Your job is to sit in the living room by the window facing the yard. If you hear Daddy moving around upstairs or if you see Mommy coming down the road you're to bang on the window."

"Oh, I don't know," Esmeralda was trying to back out of the kitchen.

"Well I do," said Drucilla switching her voice to a Grandmother Crawford imitation. "I'm in charge and you are my lookout and that is your job."

"What about Courtney?"

"He'll be your assistant."

"An assistant?" She paused in the middle of the room.

"After you've eaten your breakfast you are to go

immediately to your station," Drucilla called after her.

Esmeralda turned at the door. "Drucilla," she said angrily, "you're so bossy and pushy."

"I have to be," Drucilla said, surprised by her sister's accusation.

"Why can't you be different?"

"You mean like you?"

"Yes," Esmeralda said, smiling at the idea.

"Shy timid Esme," Drucilla said, "always gets her way without even trying."

"I just don't go pushing and bossing and scheming all the time," Esmeralda said. "It isn't nice. Mommy says it isn't the Bundage way."

"You're lucky you don't have the Bundage mouth," Drucilla said quickly, "if you did you'd give up the Bundage way, fast."

Esmeralda shrugged and walked away.

Drucilla watched her departing sister. Quiet, fair Esmeralda who made friends and didn't get into trouble could dig in her heels and not budge an inch.

Drucilla was relieved and surprised when a few minutes later Esmeralda came into the room with an armful of clothes. "Would you sell these too?" she said. "I really do hate them."

"Sure," Drucilla said happily. "Let's go outside and hang them on the rack."

Courtney came running outside to see what they

were doing. This morning Drucilla thought Courtney had his wind-up-toy look. He resembled one of his beloved stuffed animals, damp and sticky and tattered, but also motorized so that he could go and go and go and go until he dropped. "I assist, I assist," he called to Drucilla. He was very excited.

"Yes," Drucilla assured him, "you are an assistant. You are a lookout man. Esme will tell you what your duties are."

Courtney ran back into the house. "I tell the animals," he called.

When everything was arranged to her satisfaction, Drucilla went to the Nolands' to collect her poster. The Nolands were still at breakfast.

"Your parents aren't running a tag sale?" Mrs. Noland said, choking on her coffee when she looked out the window.

"No, I am," said Drucilla.

Toni hurried in barefooted. "Is this the day?" she said excitedly.

"Yes," said Drucilla. "Come over as soon as you can. I'll be in business."

She took her poster out to the mail box and set it so that it could be seen by anyone driving down the road. The sign had a picture of the human-hair wreath table under which were the words

FINE ANTIQUE TREASURES
MUST SELL
DESPERATE

Mr. and Mrs. Noland were examining the objects for sale. "Gigi," Mrs. Noland said in a concerned voice. "These are valuable things. Does your mother know about this sale?"

"My father's right upstairs," Drucilla said evasively. "And the things are mine."

"But sweetheart, this comb and brush set are worth at least seventy-five dollars."

"Then that's what I'll charge for it," said Drucilla trying to conceal her surprise. She removed the tag on which she had written five dollars. "What about that découpage chest?" she asked, realizing that she needed Mrs. Noland.

"Darling, it's a beauty. I wouldn't let it go for under a hundred. But Gigi, listen."

Drucilla didn't hear her. She was delirious. Only two hated old objects to sell and she had over a hundred and seventy-five dollars. She could practically feel her teeth being eased back. Bundage mouth, farewell.

"Gigi, do you have everything you need?" Mrs. Noland said.

"Apron, cash box," Drucilla pointed out.

"Go get a pad and pencil so you can keep track of what you've sold."

Drucilla ran into the house to get these things. "Esmeralda, Courtney, go to your station. I'm in business," she called. When she returned to the driveway she saw that a car had pulled up. A woman from Pitney Place and her two young children were circling the table. The Nolands were talking to the woman in low voices.

"Now then, here is the young lady," said Mrs. Noland loudly as Drucilla approached. "Have you got your pen and pad, Gigi?"

"Oh yes." Drucilla held them up.

"These little tables are just cunning," said the neighbor, pointing to the human-hair wreaths. "What are you asking for them?"

Drucilla looked blank. She despised the tables so much that she couldn't think of anyone seriously offering to buy them for money.

"You know, Jessie," Mrs. Noland boomed, "the stores are getting about a hundred for this stuff now. Since Gigi knows you aren't a dealer or anything, I think . . ." she looked at Drucilla. "Didn't you say you wanted seventy-five apiece, Gigi?"

"Seventy-five each?" Drucilla croaked. "Oh yes."

"Each," Mrs. Noland said emphatically.

"Well, I don't have that kind of money on me,"

the woman said. "I guess I'll discuss it with my husband, and anyway I'd just want one." She pulled her child away from the table. "Don't touch, Dwayne." The little boy had been fingering one of the detested gremlins. "How much are those?" The woman pointed to the doll.

"Four dollars each," Mrs. Noland sang out. "They

don't make those things anymore and they'll only increase in value."

"It's losing its stuffing," the woman said.

"So what, Jessie. You and I know that doesn't affect the value."

"Mmmm okay." She opened her purse and withdrew four singles. "Take the dolly, Dwayne, and be careful. It's yours, but it's also mine."

As they were backing out of the drive another car was swinging in, followed by a couple on foot.

"You folks having a tag sale so soon?" Mary Lou and Alice's mother, Mrs. Popick, called from her car. "Goodness, you just moved in."

"It's my sale," said Drucilla.

"Take a look at the little tables with the wreaths," said the woman pulling out. "If we each take one maybe we could get a better deal."

Mr. and Mrs. Popick had stepped out of their car and were looking at this and that. "Oh come see this, Jack," Mrs. Popick called to her husband. "One of those grotesque Victorian things made of human hair."

"The hair was my second cousin Muffin Egli's," said Drucilla, hoping to make the table seem even more grotesque.

"Fancy that," said Mrs. Popick.

"Awful hair," said Mr. Popick. "No wonder she yanked it out."

"It was cut off by her Aunt Cora London," said Drucilla. "She's the one who made the wreaths."

"I'm glad she's not in my family," said Mr. Popick. "I need every strand I've got." He covered his balding head with both hands and grinned. "Why are you doing this, Gigi?" he said.

"I hate them," said Drucilla. "I hate the tables too and I'd rather have braces so I can close my mouth."

"I'd like to buy them from you because I really love the awful things," said Mr. Popick. "And I'd love them even more knowing if I buy them they'll help you to be able to close your mouth. I went through the same thing when I was your age." He took out his wallet.

"Seventy-five apiece," said Drucilla.

"Will you take a check?"

Drucilla looked over at Mrs. Noland who nodded yes.

"A check is all right," said Drucilla. "Are you taking them both?"

"How I wish I could," said Mr. Popick. He wrote out a check for one of the tables and handed it to Drucilla just as the woman who had walked over gave her four dollars for a gremlin doll.

"How much are the antique dresses?" said Mrs. Popick.

The antique dresses were what Esmeralda had worn to school only yesterday.

"Mary Lou and Alice will love to play dress-up in these. They're all the rage."

"Ten dollars apiece," said Mrs. Noland.

"Look at it. It's adorable, precious." Mrs. Popick held up the horrid little dimity smock that Drucilla and Esmeralda had loathed in turn, and showed it to none other than Mrs. Brattles. She had come home without Drucilla even noticing. Just over her left shoulder Drucilla saw Esmeralda and Courtney banging away on the living-room window. She hadn't even heard.

Mrs. Brattles stood very still, looking first at the smock and then at Mrs. Popick then at Mrs. Noland and finally at Drucilla. "Drucilla," she said in her low voice. "Would you kindly tell me what is going on?"

"A tag sale," Drucilla answered in a sound that was mostly squeak. Out of the corner of her eye she saw Esmeralda's and Courtney's terrified faces watching from the kitchen door.

Mrs. Noland went up to Mrs. Brattles. "I didn't think you knew, Cordelia, so I've been watching it. She sold two of those dolls for four dollars apiece and one of those tables for seventy-five. I think the prices are fair."

"If there is to be a price," Mrs. Brattles said, "I would agree. I thank you, Mrs. Noland. I am grateful for your concern. However, we Brattleses do not sell our things. Drucilla knows this. At least she once knew it. I am afraid that Pitney Place has made her forget. I am also afraid that I shall have to conclude this little . . . tag sale." She turned her hurt and wondering gaze on Drucilla. "Take down the signs and then come with me. Your sale is over."

Drucilla went to bring in the poster. For the first time she had taken her own life in her own two hands and had done something about it.

Following her mother's straight shoulders up the front steps and through the door, she vowed to remember.

# Chapter SEVEN

Upstairs in her parents' bedroom, with her father listening sleepily from the bed, Drucilla heard Mrs. Brattles describe her return home.

"If Mrs. Duncan hadn't come in to the library to inform me that she had driven past our house and noticed a tag sale in progress, we might well have found ourselves without a stick of furniture left."

"I was only selling my own things and some of Esmeralda's," Drucilla said.

"But they aren't yours. They are family things."

"We have too many of them and I would rather have pretty teeth."

"Teeth again." Mrs. Brattles threw up her hands. "This business of her teeth is all she thinks about."

"Wait a minute, Cordelia," Mr. Brattles said. "Drucilla has mentioned her teeth so many times. It *is* important."

"It is important that she learn to make it mean less, and that we help her to realize that having straight teeth is not the key to a happy life."

"They call me Bugs Bunny at school, and draw funny pictures of me and say 'What's up, Doc?' I can't close my mouth, I can't smile," Drucilla said very quickly.

Mr. Brattles sat upright on the bed. There was no color in his cheeks. His brows drew together. "This *is* important, Cordelia," he said. Where large family questions were involved, it was always Mr. Brattles who seemed to make the final decision. It had been Mr. Brattles who had told them they had to leave Coves Landing. It was Mr. Brattles who had selected Pitney Place. He looked to Drucilla as if he were about to make a decision.

Mrs. Brattles sank onto a chair by the window. She took a long look at Drucilla. Her anger seemed to slip away. "Yes," she agreed, "I suppose it is. But I'm not sure how . . ." Her voice trailed off and Drucilla was surprised to see her usually outspoken, opinionated mother without anything more to say.

"My human-hair tables could get seventy-five dollars apiece. There are other things I can sell besides."

"Orthodontia costs a fortune," Mrs. Brattles said. "We are still in debt. But that is beside the point." She was no longer speechless—she remembered her point. "The point is, we do not sell our beloved things."

"They are not 'beloved' by ME," Drucilla said, her voice rising. "I hate them, and if I could sell them and make enough to pay for one straight tooth, I would, I would." Then Drucilla did something Bundage-Brattles girls never did. She stamped her foot. Her father told her to go immediately to her room and to stay there until told to come out.

"What do I do with my money?" Drucilla said at the door.

"Keep it for the time being," said Mrs. Brattles gravely.

"It comes to eighty-three dollars," Drucilla said. She went to her room and sat on her bed holding the cash box. She counted through the money again and tried to hear what her parents were saying down the hall. Their conversation went back and forth for some time. The tone was serious, but Drucilla could not make out the words. Drucilla looked at the empty spots where the bedside tables had stood. She leaned her head against the window. She saw Esmeralda and Courtney gathering her unsold items and bringing them into the house. She saw the Nolands standing on their lawn. Toni was holding the sign. She saw the sky begin to darken. It had been so sunny only a few minutes before, but the day had suddenly changed. Stormy inside as well as out. Mrs. Noland looked up and held out a hand to test for raindrops. Then she went into the house, holding Didi's hand. Mr. Noland, Toni, and Geri followed her. Drucilla heard Esmeralda and Courtney downstairs. They were in the foyer. Courtney was pleading to be taken someplace in the vehicle. Esmeralda was explaining that Drucilla was upstairs and couldn't drive. Courtney began to wail. Mrs. Brattles went downstairs to see what was wrong. Then she tapped on Drucilla's door.

Mrs. Brattles took a few steps into her room. "You can go downstairs now, Drucilla. Take Courtney and Esmeralda for a ride in the vehicle." She paused, looking uncomfortable and confused. "And Drucilla . . . I didn't know, we didn't realize how hard it's been for you at the new school. I'm glad you told us. It's important that you tell about those things. I guess I've been so busy with the move and my new job that I wasn't aware of what was happening. I'm sorry, Drucilla"—she reached out her hand —"*Gigi,* if I've been harsh. It was not intentional." Then her eye fell upon the empty spot where the bedside table had been and her expression changed again. "But you should not have gone ahead with that sale until you had our permission. That was wrong."

When her mother had left, Drucilla got off her bed. The dark clouds began to pour thick drops which pounded against her window.

She found Courtney and Esmeralda waiting in the back seat of the vehicle. Courtney had his animals on his lap. Esmeralda was holding two pots and a box of gingersnaps. Aunt Marianna Richard's telephone table was in place. Silently Drucilla sat herself in the driver's seat and pressed the tennis ball that was the accelerator.

"Are we going to Wits' End today?" Courtney asked.

"We are," Drucilla said.

"Will we have adventures along the way?"

"We will," Drucilla said. "We will pass through the Forest of Ferocious Things. Terrible Things."

"What sort of Things?" Courtney grew pale.

"Cupboards and bureaus and highboys and lowboys and credenzas," said Drucilla in her most forceful Grandmother Crawford imitation. "Sets of china and bowls brought from England and silver made in Boston. The chandeliers will attack from above and the gun cabinets will fire on us. We'll have to be very careful so the THINGS don't get us. It's WAR."

"Oh Drucilla," Esmeralda wailed in joyful anguish. "You make it sound so horrible."

"It is horrible," Drucilla snarled. "Make no mistake about it. The things are dangerous and they are out to get us."

"But why?" Esmeralda looked bewildered and scared. "Why are they out to get us? What have we done?"

"For one thing, they know I hate them," Drucilla said.

"Why do you hate them?" Courtney whispered.

"Because, because." Drucilla wheeled around in her seat with such force, she nearly upset the vehicle. "If we could get rid of them they would make us enough money to buy me braces and then I would have nice teeth and horrible people couldn't tease me. Because, if we sold them we could have patches on the roof and new clothes and normal furniture and rugs, like other people, and that's enough." She turned back to drive.

"Should we eat some gingersnaps to get up our strength?" said Esmeralda, who always ate when she was nervous.

"We better," said Drucilla.

They ate the cookies as the sounds of rain grew

louder against the window and the door. It became a steady, constant downpour. When the first drops fell on their heads they were not surprised.

"Is it the waterfall?" said Courtney.

"No," Drucilla said. "It's the chandelier beginning to attack."

"I'll have nightmares," Esmeralda threatened.

Drucilla squinted through her plastic windshield. "We better duck because I see a highboy trying to throw its handles at us. They're big brass ones." They all ducked, but the only thing that happened was Mrs. Brattles calling through the blanket.

"My dear children, you are sitting in the middle of one of the leaks. You'll be drenched."

They had to get out of the vehicle and run for pots and bowls and set them in all the spots to catch the dripping water. Soon the house was filled with the pinging-ponging sounds of water dripping into things. By the time they sat down to lunch, Mrs. Brattles had only one pot left.

They sat around the kitchen table in grim silence.

Finally Mr. Brattles sneezed and said, "This is awful. It's like having no roof at all."

"The people who lived here before us did say the roof needed mending," Mrs. Brattles remembered.

"The roof," said Mr. Brattles, "needs a new roof. We have got to get it one."

"With what?" said Mrs. Brattles. "We are still in debt."

Once again they were silent.

Drucilla said "ahem," and held up her fork. "Mrs. Noland said that just one of Aunt Marianna Richard's telephone tables would be a new roof over our heads and two would get us a secondhand car besides."

"Mrs. Noland seems to be your new idol," said Mrs. Brattles. "Bundages and Brattleses do not have tag sales and sell their family things, Drucilla. I am not Mrs. Noland."

Drucilla kept her eyes on her cup. "I like Mrs. Noland," she said. "Toni is my best friend. They aren't like Bundages and Brattleses but they are like most other people."

Mrs. Brattles stopped eating. Her eyes grew large and sad. She turned to her husband. "See what has happened, Winston? She is ashamed of us. She thinks we're different, and one way or another in this place, I suppose we are." She rested her forehead on her palm. "I wish I knew what to do," she said.

All afternoon it rained. Drucilla, Esmeralda, and Courtney had moved the vehicle to a dry corner of the foyer. It took them a long time to move all the parts and set it up again. When the job was done,

Mrs. Brattles called for them to help dump the pots of water. After that they sat on the damp threadbare Oriental rug in the living room and listened to Mr. Brattles telephone a roofer. Half an hour later the man was standing in the foyer. He said he would start work on their roof early the following week.

When the dinner dishes had been put away, Drucilla heard her father on the telephone saying, "It's the little round table, Mrs. Noland, the one you saw the children using as a steering wheel. We call them telephone tables because my aunt used them as that, but of course they predate the telephone by many years. My wife told me that you did a quick appraisal of the table that day you dropped in." He listened in silence for a moment and then his brows lifted in surprise. "You don't say. *That* much?" He listened again very attentively and made an appointment to see Mrs. Noland the following day. After he hung up he told Mrs. Brattles what Mrs. Noland had said. Mrs. Brattles didn't say anything at first. She just walked into the living room and rearranged some of the pots to catch water better. She stood very still in the middle of the room staring out the darkened window. "This afternoon I said I wished I knew what to do," she murmured, "and now . . . I know what to do. Change a little, bend a little. We aren't at Coves Landing anymore. We're here in

Pitney Place. A new house, new people, and some new ways of thinking."

Mrs. Brattles began to move about the room slowly, seeing each piece of furniture as if for the first time. She looked at the sofa, the chairs, the cabinets and the butler's tray table, the sideboard and the bookcases. Then she studied the portraits on the walls. There was an odd intense light in her eyes.

When tornadoes or floods or fires threaten, they are preceded by a warning. The light in Mrs. Brattles's eye was just such a warning. Like a sharp drop in temperature, a rising tide, or the smell of smoke, it meant they were all in for some very big changes.

# Chapter EIGHT

The next morning was clear and chilly. The drenched sidewalks showed patches where they had begun to dry. Wet leaves formed mounds on the driveways. It was nine-thirty when Mrs. Noland rang the door bell. She was wearing a tweed suit, stockings, and shoes with small wooden heels. She looked like a Bundage or a Brattles from Coves Landing. She carried a little leather briefcase and the expression on her face was very businesslike. "Good morning, good morning," she said brightly as her heels clicked across the foyer tiles. "I see you've been rained on again." Her eye took in the last of the pots.

"I hope this isn't an inconvenience," Mrs. Brattles began.

"An inconvenience? My dear Mrs. B, this is my work. I love it, especially when it involves a treasure trove of these dimensions." She waved her hand to encompass the room. "Now tell me what you want to sell, and I'll tell you what you can hope to get for it and how to proceed."

And so they went into the living room and Mrs. Noland examined this and that with her sharp appraising eyes and made notations in her notebook and from time to time looked something up in one of her reference books or catalogues. Then she sat down carefully on the sofa and did some figuring and showed the figures to Mr. and Mrs. Brattles.

When Mrs. Brattles saw the figures in Mrs. Noland's book, she didn't say a word.

Slowly she looked around the room again. "That would mean a new roof as well as getting out of debt with money to spare." She sighed. "I do thank you, Mrs. Noland. Proceed if you will with the arrangements for the sale of the tables."

After Mrs. Noland left, Mrs. Brattles avoided looking at the portrait of Aunt Marianna Richard. "I wonder what she would make of it," she said nervously. "Do you think she would understand?"

"I do," Drucilla blurted. "She would say, 'Good riddance.' " Drucilla said this in the high commanding voice she used to imitate Grandmother Bundage. Both her parents laughed at the imitation. "She would say, 'Get a nice new roof over your heads, Cordelia, and if there's any money left over, for heaven's sake buy Drucilla some braces.' "

Mrs. Brattles stopped laughing. "Your teeth. That's where all this began. Daddy and I are beginning to see your point."

Drucilla could not believe her ears.

Her father nodded. "As soon as we can, we will arrange to get you braces."

Mrs. Brattles sighed resignedly, but Drucilla didn't care. She was happy. She had won.

* * *

When Drucilla came home from school on Monday, the tables were gone. The roofer and his crew were up on the roof.

"What will we do for a steering wheel?" Courtney asked.

"We'll make one out of cardboard," Drucilla said. She had thought about this already. She and Esmeralda cut the steering wheel out of cardboard and made the shaft out of a paper-towel roller. They fitted it into the vehicle. It wasn't nearly as sturdy as the table had been and the vehicle looked less substantial, but it worked.

"Are we going for an adventure?" said Courtney.

"Not today," Drucilla said. Too many things were happening in the house. Toni had invited her for the afternoon. They planned to swap clothes and play with some new paper dolls. Anyway she hadn't thought up the next adventure for the journey to Wits' End. It was obvious that they had won the war with the THINGS. The new steering wheel was proof of that.

At Toni's house, wearing one of Toni's permanent-pleated skirts and cutting out Toni's new Hollywood Stars Paper Dolls, Drucilla forgot about the events at home until Toni said, "Your mother was over here this morning. Guess what? Now she's thinking about selling your sofa. She was all upset about it, but she said it was a question of 'priorities.' She said, 'People are more important than things.' And she said she had to consider 'human needs.' "

"I think that's my teeth," Drucilla said.

"My mother says if she sells the sofa, you people will be on easy street."

"Easy Street?" Drucilla repeated. It had an ominous sound.

That night at dinner Mrs. Brattles was very excited. Her eyes shone and her voice was high. "Oh what a day," she began. "The tables were picked up. I put the check in the bank. The roofers came. I called a carpenter and a plumber. There is a lot of work to be done in this house. The roofer told me it was necessary to get it done before the problems get worse." She seemed surprised. "Winston, I never thought I would do this."

Mr. Brattles reached over and took her hand. "They would understand, Cordelia. Times change. People change. The world doesn't stand still. We must move with it, or we are left behind." Then he chuckled. "To tell the truth, I don't miss those tables one bit."

"It is nice to think that the house is tight," Mrs. Brattles said. "Such a relief to know it can rain and rain. I love that feeling." She looked over at her aunt's portrait. "I agree with you, I think she does understand." They were all silent for a few moments and then Mrs. Brattles said, "Tell me, do you think Grandmother would object if we sold her carpets and chairs for that new drainage system? Do you think she would be happy for us to enjoy some plumbing repairs? Good water pressure and unclogged pipes?" She waited a moment before answering her own question. "I think she would."

It had begun, the worst week Drucilla had yet known at Pitney Place. On Tuesday afternoon, returning from school with Toni and the twins, Drucilla looked down the street toward her house and gasped. There were two trucks parked in the Brattleses' driveway. One of them said Brink Plumbing and Heating on its side, the other was open and the credenza was being hauled into it.

"What a funny piece of furniture," Alice said.

"It's called a credenza," said Drucilla, embarrassed for the dignified piece of furniture being caught with its bowed legs up in the air. "We kept it in the dining room. It held tablecloths, napkins, and silver."

"There are no dining rooms at Pitney Place," said Mary Lou. The twins lived in the same model house as Drucilla.

"That was the problem," said Drucilla. The workmen had gotten the credenza into the truck. She could tell there were other familiar pieces of furniture inside.

"Can we see your house?" Alice said. "You never invite us."

"I can't today," said Drucilla. "I have to study for the math test."

"Then tomorrow," said Alice.

"Okay, tomorrow."

Drucilla had been putting the twins off for days. She knew she would have to have them soon. She was not entirely fibbing about having to study math. She was completely lost in the subject. The school at Pitney Place had covered work which she had never had at Coves Landing. Also she had been teased more than usual at lunch. She wanted to be alone. She waved good-bye and went immediately to the kitchen. She had been looking forward to her tall glass of cold milk, plate of Mallomars, and the peace of the kitchen. But in the kitchen she found a plumber sprawled on the floor investigating the bottom of the sink, tapping and banging and muttering. Drucilla poured out her milk, placed the glass on a tray with the box of cookies, and headed for the living room and the old sofa where she could curl up and munch and sip and daydream in its comforting smelly depths. When she got to the living room she found the sofa was gone. She stared at the empty spot where it had been and remembered that it was what she had seen already loaded into the truck in the driveway. She went to the kitchen and poured the milk back into the container. She could not have swallowed a thing.

The next afternoon Alice and Mary Lou and Toni came home with her.

"I failed the test, I know I did," Mary Lou said for the sixth time as they turned down Drucilla's path.

"You always say that and then you get an eighty-

five," Alice said. "I'm the one who never says it and I'm the one who fails."

"I really did this time," Mary Lou promised. "Oh look, Gigi, there's a carpenter's truck outside your place today."

Inside the house was bedlam. Doors were off their hinges, and windows removed from their frames lay against the walls. A carpenter and his assistant hammered and sanded and planed. The scream of the electric saw or drill sounded intermittently. Drucilla led her guests over the mounds of sawdust and piles of tools to the kitchen. Surrounded by heaps of antique catalogues and furniture texts, sipping tea and munching cinnamon toast, sat Mrs. Noland and Mrs. Brattles.

"Some changes around here, aren't there, Gigi?" Mrs. Noland said cheerily.

Drucilla nodded.

"We've just arranged to sell the dining-room set for a small fortune," Mrs. Brattles said. "And the Oriental rugs so we can lay wall-to-wall carpets. Toni, your mother is not only a genius but the best friend I ever had."

"Oh Cordy," Mrs. Noland protested.

"But it's true," said Mrs. Brattles earnestly. "You've changed my life, Peg. You and Dru—un—Gigi."

Drucilla set out milk for her friends and put a plate of gingersnaps on a tray. She led them through the back door to the kitchen steps where they could sit down in relative quiet.

"Your house sure has changed," Toni said morosely.

Drucilla nodded. "So has my mother."

"It's very noisy," said Alice. "Can we see the portraits and old stuff?"

"Whatever is left," Drucilla said.

After she showed them around, Toni suggested they all go over to her house. They did so gratefully.

When Drucilla came home late in the afternoon, the workmen had left and the house was quiet. Mrs. Brattles was working over her checkbook at the kitchen table. Mr. Brattles, home from his office, was helping Esmeralda with her math homework and Courtney was banging a carrot stick on a pot cover. Mrs. Brattles set down her pen and removed her glasses. "Drucilla dear," she said. "I'm glad you're here for my important announcement."

Courtney stopped banging and Esmeralda stopped adding.

"We are out of debt. We don't owe anybody anything anymore," Mrs. Brattles said.

"Then we don't have to sell any more of our things?" Drucilla said.

"Oh but Drucilla dear, your braces," Mrs. Brattles protested. "And there's so much else besides."

For the first time Drucilla grew frightened. She *did* want braces but she didn't like the way the house was changing. Too many things were gone. There were sad empty spots where furniture had been. She never knew she would miss the old sofa. Now she missed the credenza as well, but mostly she missed the old Cordelia Brattles. She had wanted her mother to change. Now that she had, it was as if the world had turned upside down.

On Thursday afternoon Drucilla and Esmeralda stood waiting for their mother to pick them up outside the school. Chrissy strode up to them. "Where are you going today?" she said to Drucilla.

"My mother is picking us up to take us shopping."

Chrissy's eyes widened. "For socks and underwear?"

"No, dresses."

"What about The Old Book Look?"

"I guess it's all over," Drucilla said glumly. As much as she longed for normal clothes, she hated letting Chrissy know it.

"I can't wait to see what you get," Chrissy said. For the first time Drucilla thought she meant it.

"Youuuuu hooooo," Mrs. Brattles called from the car.

They drove to a large shopping mall. All the way Mrs. Brattles chatted gaily about her plans. She was going to make a tea party for the new neighbors at Pitney Place. They had a lot to celebrate. She would buy invitations and some paper napkins. "You girls could use a few new things for once in your life," she went on. "It's wonderful to meet new people and buy new things. I used to have so much trouble, I hardly knew what to say unless somebody was in the family. But now I have so many friends."

On the Young World floor of a large store Mrs. Brattles told a saleswoman, "We'd like to see some outfits for these two girls. Show us bright happy clothes for both school and Thanksgiving." They bought shirts and skirts and pullovers and dress-up shoes and dress-up dresses and jackets and sweaters. Mrs. Brattles kept saying, "Don't bother to choose, you can use them all."

When the new clothes had been wrapped up Mrs. Brattles sighed happily. "There, now, that's done." Then she took a note pad out of her purse and as she checked things off on it thought out loud, "I wonder if we have time to go to kitchen wares. I could use a new table and some nice new kitchen

chairs and a few pots with handles and covers to match." Then she looked at her wristwatch. "I guess it's time to go home, but tomorrow is another day. I've decided to get rid of the gun cabinet and some of the silver. What a joy to be finished with all that polishing."

The next day was Friday. Drucilla wore her orange pants and yellow pullover. The first person to see her was Toni. "Oh Gigi," she cried. "You look like everybody else."

When they got to school Alice said dimly, "I have those, they're on sale at the mall."

"Now you look like us," Chrissy said.

It turned out to be the first day that no one teased her. When she came home she found that a soft new carpet had been laid clear from the foyer through the living room right up to the kitchen tiles. It was blue.

At dinner Mrs. Brattles told Drucilla that she had made an appointment for her to see the orthodontist the following week. "It's about time," she said. "They say if you start young you can change things before they get too set." She tapped her own teeth wistfully. "Like mine." Then she shrugged. "Come help me address invitations."

"Invitations?"

"To my tea party. I'd like you and your sister to give me a hand with the serving and preparation too."

They sat down on the soft blue rug in the living room and wrote names and addresses on the envelopes. Everything her mother did now filled Drucilla with alarm. She even dreaded the tea party.

# Chapter NINE

"Come right in," Mrs. Brattles called gaily to the group of ladies she had invited to tea. "So glad you could all come. I've been wanting to ask my Pitney Place neighbors ever since we moved, but it's taken ever so long to set things right here. Just set your boots in the Bootique." She pointed to a bright plastic tray on the floor. "Let me have your coats so I can put them on the bed inside. Please go into the living room and make yourself comfortable. Drucilla, Esmeralda, help me with the coats."

Drucilla took as many coats as she could carry and followed her mother into the bedroom where she set them down on the bed.

Mrs. Brattles had been planning this tea party for days. She had gotten the names of all her neighbors at Pitney Place, bought a box of little invitations, baked up a dazzling array of tiny cakes, and sliced up a number of cucumbers for thin little sandwiches. She had arranged the cakes and sandwiches on two of Grandmother Eliot's silver trays. The tea was to be brewed in the silver pot with the ivory stand. The cups and saucers and cake plates were Bundage family Lowestoft, handed down for generations. Everything was set. The living room could easily hold the ladies of Pitney Place now since it was practically empty of furniture. There were the bookcases, the butler's tray table, two chairs and a new foam rubber shelf they called the sofa. The ladies filed into the room staring and commenting on this and that. Mrs. Nolan had brought Toni on condition that she would help Drucilla and Esmeralda serve and clean up.

"What wonderful old portraits," Mary Lou's mother said. "They must be worth a fortune."

Mrs. Brattles smiled and nodded. "You know, until we moved here to Pitney Place, I hadn't an idea in the world about the value of anything. But Peg Noland has changed all that. If you had told me a month ago that those portraits were worth anything I'd have said, 'Don't be silly.' Now that I'm no longer ignorant I can tell you that you are absolutely right. The antiques catalogue puts those portraits at six hundred dollars apiece. I could hardly believe it." Drucilla came by with her tray. "Won't you try a sandwich? The cucumber are very good."

Mary Lou's mother selected a sandwich and settled on the edge of the sofa. "How do you like living at Pitney Place?" she asked.

Mrs. Brattles sat beside her and took a deep breath. "I love it," she said emphatically.

"Oh tell us why," said a lady on the other side of Mary Lou's mother. "Sometimes I wish we could move to a bigger, fancier house."

"So many wonderful things have happened since we came to live here," said Mrs. Brattles. "My husband found a job he likes and so have I. But even better than that, I've broken out of so many old habits. I've changed my way of thinking about a lot of things. I've learned a lot. It's been so exciting. Of course I don't know if all these things would have happened without Peggy Noland."

Mrs. Noland bowed her head and smiled. "Come now, Cordy," she said. "You were ready for some changes."

"I guess Druc—Gigi had started the wheels turning, Peggy, but I wouldn't have had the nerve without you."

"Nerve for what?" Mrs. Lopate and the other women looked confused.

"To sell some of our old family pieces to put us back on our feet," Mrs. Brattles said candidly.

"I see," Mrs. Crowly said slowly as the idea dawned on her. "You mean these old pieces are for sale? This butler's tray table, for instance?"

"I suppose so," Mrs. Brattles said.

"It's a beauty," Mrs. Lopate picked up her plate to inspect the veneer. "I have a copy, but this is different."

"It's authentic all right," Mrs. Brattles assured her.

"I've never seen so many beautiful antiques in one house," Mrs. Borganza said.

Mrs. Lopate was still inspecting the tray table. "Everything we have is a copy. It's nice to see the real thing."

"I've been told that buying antique furniture is a good investment," Mrs. Brattles said. "Better than stocks because you get to use and enjoy what you've bought." She stood up to pour the tea. "If we hadn't been beset by such urgent money problems I would have happily dusted these things for the rest of my days."

Drucilla couldn't help but give her mother a sideways look as she and Toni began to pass the tray of cakes.

"What a beautiful silver tray," Mrs. Lopate remarked excitedly, helping herself to a pastry. "Has it a hallmark? Oh I do love silver. Now don't tell me you'd part with it, Cordy."

"But of course I would."

"Could you give me a ball-park figure?"

"Peggy's got the catalogue and we use those figures as a guide."

"I'm definitely interested. Please let me know."

"I surely will."

"Is this Lowestoft?" Mrs. Brady eyed her teacup.

"Family heirloom," Mrs. Brattles said.

"Would you let it go piecemeal? I mean, could I pick up a cup and saucer? I collect them. Odd ones. I have a cupboard full of them," Mrs. Crowly explained.

As she circled the room with cups and sandwiches it seemed to Drucilla that the guests were noticing everything around them as if they were in a shop.

"I will have to consult the catalogue," Mrs. Brattles kept repeating. "I might consider dismantling the set of china. I'm not sure."

"If you decide to, would you let me know?" a dark-haired neighbor piped. "I'd love a few serving bowls in this pattern."

"Say, would you part with that silver tea service?" a Mrs. Tindle wanted to know.

Before Mrs. Brattles could answer, Mrs. Brady interrupted, "What about the portraits? They certainly do class up a room."

Drucilla gazed at the sad eyes of Great-grandmother Bundage and then quickly looked away.

"The portraits are definitely on the market," Mrs. Brattles said.

Then all in a rush and all together everyone in the room was talking at once. What about the miniatures and the wine table and the darling little wig stand?

Mrs. Brattles could scarcely answer the questions, they were flying so fast between sips of tea. Out of the blue Toni Noland began to laugh. She laughed so hard she started to choke.

"What is it, Toni?" Mrs. Noland patted her back.

"Oh Mom," Toni said, "if Gigi's in the catalogue d'you suppose Mrs. Brattles would sell her to us at dealer's price?"

There was an awkward silence which Peggy Noland filled with a few sharp peals of nervous laughter. "You silly," she said, "you know perfectly well that if Gigi were in the catalogue we'd snap her up at any price."

A few of the women chuckled. Cordelia Brattles's face broke out in red splotches. "I guess we all got carried away," she murmured.

A Mrs. Diamond broke the silence that followed by asking for the recipe for the pastry tarts and Mrs. Brattles gave it to her. "It's free of charge," she said, trying to make a joke of the whole thing.

Soon the ladies were standing about, putting on their coats and struggling into their boots and saying

"Good-bye" and "Thank you" and "We'll be in touch," and Mrs. Brattles was waving from her door.

Drucilla, Toni, and Esmeralda helped to clear the tea things and take them into the kitchen. In a hushed voice Toni said, "I'm sorry I said that, Gigi, about buying you. But I was beginning to think it might happen and the idea really cracked me up."

"Don't be sorry." Drucilla shook her head. "It is funny, and it's my fault."

"What do you mean your fault?"

"I was the one who wanted to sell our things, remember? I made the tag sale and screamed for braces and new clothes. I was ashamed and I wanted to be like everybody else at Pitney Place." She thought for a moment as the idea came to her. "Now Mom's doing the same thing."

At dinner Mrs. Brattles excitedly reported to her husband about the tea party. "I thought I was just giving a nice welcoming get-together," she said, "but Winston, you wouldn't believe what happened. Everybody got into a buying mood. Someone wanted the butler's tray table, someone else made me an offer for the china cups, and a few people are interested in the silver tea service."

"What will you do about all these offers?" Mr. Brattles asked cheerfully.

"I said I'd have to wait and check them against the catalogue prices."

"Say, Cordy," Mr. Brattles said, "you've gotten awfully good at this."

Mrs. Brattles bowed her head happily, to receive the compliment.

Drucilla had hoped that her father would raise some objection, but he seemed as enthusiastic as her mother.

"You know, Winston, I've been thinking," Mrs. Brattles began. "We've been selling off the big bulky old pieces and the small valuable ones, but we have so many odds and ends that are neither here nor there. Wouldn't it be great fun to gather them all together and run a garage sale some nice weekend before Christmas?"

"Good idea," Mr. Brattles said.

Esmeralda said, "A tag sale, just like Drucilla's."

Mr. and Mrs. Brattles burst out laughing. "Yes, we owe that one to Drucilla," Mrs. Brattles said.

Drucilla excused herself from the table and wandered miserably into the foyer. Courtney followed close behind her.

"Are we going to Wits' End?" he said.

"I don't know."

"Well, why not?" He pulled her into the vehicle. "Don't we know where we want to go?"

Suddenly she did know. "I want to go back," Drucilla said. "I want to go back to when we had the old furniture and Mommy said, 'We are Brattleses and we value our old things.' " She thought with yearning of the patterned Oriental rugs, of the credenza with its great varnished front ballooning out over spindly bowed legs. And the sofa so deep and awkward and full of that funny smell of ages. She thought she had hated that smell, but it was also the smell of home. The Nolands' sofa had no smell. Nobody's sofa smelled like that graceful piece of furniture. She thought with longing of her mother, proudly defending their odd family ways right down to their family mouth.

We Brattleses, we Bundages, we come from someplace, we care about our traditions. The new Mrs. Brattles had forgotten. Drucilla knew that she had started it all with her plans. Then it came to her. She could make another plan. She would make a plan to go back before it was too late. She would think up some way to stop the tag sale or garage sale and make them remember who they were.

She put her hand down on the new steering wheel and waited for a brainstorm, but none came.

# Chapter TEN

No idea came in the days that followed either. Drucilla spent hours driving Courtney and his animals to Wits' End, trying to think up some wonderful way to get back to a time and place she could hardly describe.

Walking to school with Esmeralda the week before Thanksgiving, she blurted, "Isn't it awful what's happened to Mom?"

"What are you talking about?" said Esmeralda, alarmed.

"Don't you see how she's changed? And Daddy too?"

"Yes, and I love it," Esmeralda said.

"But it's too much," Drucilla insisted. "Don't you wish she would go back to the way she was?"

"I like my new clothes," Esmeralda said emphatically. "I won't give them up."

"I don't mean you should give up your clothes," said Drucilla.

"Then what do you mean?"

"The furniture and the dishes and all the other things."

"I love the furniture," Esmeralda said, "and the carpet wall to wall to wall to wall. Oh I love it. Anyway you started it all, Drucilla."

Drucilla sighed. "I know, I know."

"Hey, Gigi," Chipper called from the other side of the road.

For a moment Drucilla's stomach turned over but nothing happened. Chipper had stopped teasing her. He and Brucie were involved in baseball. They had never even commented on her braces. Toni and Chrissy ran up behind her.

"Why didn't you wait for me?" Toni called.

"I thought you had left," Drucilla said.

"No, I was helping Mom pick a recipe for the stuffing. Are you going to be around for Thanksgiving?"

"We're going back to Coves Landing," Drucilla said.

"And I'll wear my new wash-and-wear pleats and my patent leather shoes," Esmeralda added.

"Big thrill," Chrissy said.

"It is a big thrill for us," Drucilla said in her sister's defense.

"And what'll you wear?" Chrissy wanted to know.

"I'm not sure yet," Drucilla lied. She knew perfectly well. She had picked everything out down to the last detail. She lay awake nights thinking about the trip back to Coves Landing and how it would be. She prayed that seeing the family again would make her parents remember who they were.

Thanksgiving morning the Brattles family was in a state. Mrs. Brattles had decided to wear her old good wool dress. It was a heather tweed made of indestructible wool. She had bought it in London on her honeymoon. Preparation for the Thanksgiving trip put a halt to preparations for the garage sale scheduled to take place the following weekend. "People will be thinking about Christmas," Mrs. Brattles had said in her new lisp, for she too had braces. She had gotten them a few days after Drucilla, saying, "Drucilla was quite right. There is no reason why we have to go through life with Bundage teeth if something can be done about it." Drucilla, who was quoted more and more frequently, could not admit how upset she was at the thought of her mother's mouth being changed.

At ten-thirty in the morning they all piled into Mr. Brattles's car. As they drove along the highway, Drucilla gazed out the window into the gray overcast day, wondering what the Coves Landing cousins would make of them (not to mention the aunts and uncles). It seemed they had been gone for years, not three months.

Mrs. Brattles must have been thinking the same thing. She was scratching away at her arms. "This dress is killing me," she said. "I forgot how it itches. I really couldn't wear my new suit. Mother and Aunt Lucinda would be horrified." Then she chewed on her finger nervously. "Oh Winston, if they knew what we've been doing."

"What if they knew? It's our business what we do with our things." Mr. Brattles said these brave words without much conviction. Drucilla noted that there was no color in his cheeks and his brow was furrowed.

Coves Landing was a five-hour drive from Pitney Place. Drucilla fell asleep and dreamed she was in the vehicle on her way to Wits' End. She dreamed the vehicle got lost and Courtney got sick and started to cry and Esmeralda said there was no Wits'

End. Then she woke up because Courtney *was* crying. He couldn't find one of the animals and feared he had left it behind and it would never forgive him for missing Thanksgiving. Mrs. Brattles was trying to soothe him. "We'll buy you a new panda," she said.

"No, I want old panda," Courtney wailed.

"Old panda is so grubby," Mrs. Brattles said. "He's too old."

"Noo!" Courtney was horrified. "He's my old panda."

Just then they were distracted because they were approaching Coves Landing. They had passed the drugstore and the beauty shop and were turning into the final road. Coves Landing was near the sea. Their noses filled with the smell of ocean that had always been home to them. They hadn't noticed how they had missed it. In ten minutes they were driving by the large Brattles and Bundage houses. The houses were well back from the road behind screens of pine and oak. Mr. Brattles turned into the winding driveway of Aunt Lucinda's house. As they rounded the circular drive they could see familiar faces in the downstairs windows. The front door was flung open by Aunt Lucinda herself. Grandmother Bundage was at her side. Soon everyone was greeting excitedly. There were comments about how

Courtney had grown, but no one said a word on the subject of braces or "plastic clothes." That was just like the family. They didn't come right out with things. Drucilla and Esmeralda took their overnight bags and went upstairs with their cousins Blakesly, Daphne, and Katney. No sooner had they closed the upstairs guest room door than the three cousins began at once.

"Drucilla, what clothes! Where do you get such clothes?"

"What are your pants made of? Oh please let me see your braces. Are they terrible agony? Do you have awful rubber bands?" asked Daphne, who had the most extreme Bundage mouth of them all.

Drucilla pulled her lips back with her fingers so the braces could be inspected by all of them. "The clothes came from a shopping center near Pitney Place," she said.

"Is Pitney Place terrible? Is there anybody like us?" Blakesly asked nervously. Blakesly was the most timid of the cousins. "Did they make fun of you, Drucilla? Did they think you were strange?"

"Yes," Drucilla said. "They did think I was strange, and so did I. But now I'm not strange anymore and they've stopped teasing." No sooner had she said this than she realized that now she felt strange again. The cousins were dressed in the same old hand-me-down trunk clothes she had so detested. But much to her surprise she thought they looked very pretty and sweet in their ruffles and tucks. She felt out of place, too bright and shiny. There was a knock on the door.

Aunt Lucinda came in. "I don't want to interrupt," she said, "but when you have a free moment I would like to see you, Drucilla. I'll be down in the library with the family."

Drucilla and Esmeralda had a hundred questions to ask their cousins about the old school and friends and teachers. They changed out of their clothes and put on their party dresses and shoes. While they changed, the cousins examined their clothes.

"Will you pass these along?" Daphne said, only to realize with a pang that she was already the same size as Drucilla.

When they had changed, Drucilla and Esmeralda went downstairs. The family was sitting in the library hearing all about Pitney Place from Mr. and Mrs. Brattles. Aunt Lucinda excused herself. She took Drucilla by the hand and led her into the front room.

"Drucilla dear," she said, "I realize that your birthday falls between Thanksgiving and Christmas, at a time when I won't be able to see you. So I am going to give you your gift now. I want the pleasure of watching you open your present." She went to the little cherry wood desk by the window and from its top drawer took a small box which she gave to Drucilla.

Drucilla carefully undid the ribbon and silver paper and opened the lid. Inside the box, on a bed of blue cotton, was a gold locket, intricately etched with a pattern of leaves and flowers and set with a tiny ruby. The locket's chain was a golden thread. "Oh," Drucilla sighed, "it's beautiful. I love it. It's the one in the portrait."

"Yes. It belonged to Emily Crawford Bundage," Aunt Lucinda said. "And now it is yours."

"Thank you, Aunt Lucinda," Drucilla put her arms around her Aunt and kissed her soft powdered cheek. "I love it and will keep it forever."

"Well, for a lifetime anyway," Aunt Lucinda laughed. She helped Drucilla put the locket around her neck. "Perhaps one day your portrait will be painted while you wear it and then years later some new member of the family will look at it and say, 'That's Drucilla Brattles who was so clever and could run an organization.' "

When they returned to the library, all the relatives admired the locket. Drucilla circled the room to show it to everyone. The aunts and uncles exclaimed about it. After Aunt Susannah examined the locket she lifted her gaze to Drucilla's mouth. "Why Drucilla, what do I see? Are those braces?" She turned to Mrs. Brattles. "Cordelia, you got her braces."

"We both got braces," said Mrs. Brattles, showing a tense smile so that her own could be seen.

"They must cost a fortune," Aunt Susannah said. "I shouldn't like to imagine what the bills come to."

"They can do remarkable things these days," gentle Aunt Lucinda said. "But aren't you too old, Cordy? Don't you have to start when you're young?"

"Not necessarily," said Mrs. Brattles, pleased to be the expert. She explained very carefully what was being done in her mouth as well as Drucilla's. She told them how teeth were being eased into their proper places, how the bite would be improved and how food would be better chewed and digestion affected. The family was fascinated. As she concluded her talk on teeth, Mrs. Brattles, ever enthusiastic, said, "These braces are important for both Drucilla and myself. They come before many other things. They are worth every penny."

To Drucilla's profound dismay she saw her mother's eye fall upon the new gold locket.

"For example," Mrs. Brattles went on, "we must make choices between the old and the new, the charm of the past and the needs of the present. Our family has not been very good at making these choices." Her eyes seemed glued to the locket. Drucilla put her hand over it. Could her mother have plans for the locket? She had thought that the Thanksgiving party might make her mother stop. On the contrary, it seemed to have spurred her onward.

# Chapter ELEVEN

The drive back to Pitney Place the next morning was the gloomiest Drucilla had ever experienced. They were all tired and too full of food. There was no longer the excitement of the holiday before them. It was over. They were no longer in suspense as to what Pitney Place would be like. They knew. They also knew that they had begun to grow away from their family and that the family was aware of it. Drucilla did not look forward to anything, not school on Monday or the garage sale only one week off. She had come to think of the garage sale as a terrible ending to a sad story. She still hadn't any idea of how to stop it. Courtney began to sneeze. He had caught a cold. Esmeralda sucked on her knuckle till it was red, and her eyes looked watery. Mr. Brattles was silent and Mrs. Brattles fiddled with the dials of the radio, but couldn't get any station to come through clearly. "That's a lovely locket," she said to Drucilla. "I think it's worth a small fortune."

Drucilla's stomach pitched. "Can I open my window? I feel sick."

"Oh no, do you want us to pull over?" Mrs. Brattles groaned.

"Not yet." For the rest of the trip Drucilla had to keep rolling her window up and down (which made Courtney cough) depending on how sick she felt. As they pulled into their driveway at Pitney Place, Mr. Brattles said emphatically that it would be a long time before he made that trip again, thereby wrecking Drucilla's one pleasant hope, going back to Coves Landing for Christmas.

On Monday morning a surprising thing happened. Chrissy walked up to Drucilla and said, "Can I visit your house after school?"

Drucilla nodded yes.

"I heard about it from my mother's friend, Mrs. Diamond. She said it's like a museum of old things."

And so Drucilla knew that she had not become

suddenly popular with Chrissy. She wanted to see the things.

At lunch when the twins learned that Chrissy was going home with Drucilla they invited her to join their game of hopscotch. Drucilla felt that a small curse had been magically lifted by Chrissy's favor. But she was apprehensive about the visit. It was too sudden.

When Chrissy entered the house at Pitney Place she immediately began to inspect it. Even before going into the kitchen for a snack, she lingered in the foyer examining things. She circled the room, from the Queen Anne side table, to the shelf with the candlesticks and Meissen bowl. "How old is that?" she wanted to know of each piece. "Where did that come from?" Then she caught sight of the vehicle. "What is it?" she asked without much interest.

Drucilla told her reluctantly. She didn't want Chrissy to see her private place. Chrissy didn't seem interested in seeing it. "Uh huh. Let's look at the living room now."

And so they trooped into the living room. "Ugh," Chrissy said of the new sofa. "That's the same one we've got. The foam in ours is disintegrating. It crunches when you sit on it."

"But it didn't used to be like this," Drucilla said.

"We had another sofa that was deep and smelled and was covered in threadbare plush."

"What happened to it."

"We sold it," Drucilla said.

"How horrible." Chrissy allowed herself a frown.

"Yes it is." Drucilla actually trembled in agreement.

"Let's eat something," Chrissy said.

After glasses of milk Chrissy said she wanted to look at the vehicle. Drucilla was surprised. They settled inside the dark place. Chrissy examined the dials and switches. "You know what your house reminds me of?" she said slowly. "A few years ago my parents took me to a mansion out on Long Island. We paid a dollar each and then a guide showed us around all the rooms and told us about each piece of furniture and the rugs on the floors and even the clothes in the closet. The furniture was just like yours. It was called the Heritage Tour."

Then IT happened. Drucilla got THE IDEA. It was so obvious, so perfect, and so easy that she didn't know why it had not come to her before. She forced herself to stay calm and ask Chrissy questions about the house she had visited. "Stay right where you are, Chrissy, don't move. I just have to get a pencil and a piece of paper to write all this down."

"Hey, what's going on?"

"Just stay there." Drucilla came back with a pad and pencil. "Okay, now how long did the tour last? What did the guide talk about?"

"Wait a minute. One at a time."

Drucilla slowed down. She waited for Chrissy's answers and wrote them in her book with care.

After a while Chrissy grew bored. "Can't we finish this up? I really came over here so I could try on some of your old clothes. Toni says it's fun."

Drucilla took Chrissy up to her room, helped her into some of her oldest smocked cotton floral dresses, and then watched her gazing in admiration at her reflection in Drucilla's mirror. She said she felt exactly like someone out of an old book.

Drucilla could hardly wait for Chrissy to leave. There was so much she had to do and so little time in which to do it.

"I need your help, Esme," Drucilla whispered to her sister as they were setting the table for dinner a few hours later.

"What is it?" Esmeralda put down her handful of forks. When she heard Drucilla's scheme she put both hands over her ears. "I hate it. I won't. I don't want to hear about it. Drucilla, how could you?"

"Shhhhh," Drucilla hissed. "I need you. You've got to help me." She wanted to shake Esmeralda. She was frantic.

"It's a terrible idea. It would make Mommy upset. Anyway, I don't care if we sell our things."

"But who will we be when our things are gone?"

"We'll have other things, better ones."

"But they won't be us, our heritage."

"I don't know what that is."

"It's things that mean something, that tell a story.

My locket that's the same as the one in the portrait. It's history."

"I don't care about history."

Mrs. Brattles poked her head around the door. "What are you two whispering about?"

Esmeralda blurted, "Mommy, do you care about history?"

"Why of course I do," said Mrs. Brattles. "I loved history in school. It was my favorite subject."

"What about family history?" Drucilla said, catching her sister's I-told-you-so look.

"Yes, yes, of course."

"I mean the sort of history that means my locket is on Granny Bundage's neck in the portrait and it will be on mine and then maybe my granddaughter's years and years from now."

"Mmmm, yes dear." Mrs. Brattles looked as if she had just recollected something. "Speaking of that locket, I'm glad you reminded me. I wondered just how attached to it you have become. It's one of those things that you'll hardly ever wear and then have to worry about when you do. If you'd like to sell it, it could mean piano lessons or even a month at summer camp or a brand-new desk." She must have seen Drucilla's expression for she stopped speaking and took a step backward. "Well, give it a thought." Courtney called from the living room and she left.

They were silent for a moment. Esmeralda was placing the napkins with great care. "Drucilla, I'll help you," she said.

# Chapter TWELVE

"Courtney," Drucilla said the next night, as she stood by his bedside, "can we borrow your animals?"

In response Courtney clutched the bag to his chest and plunged his thumb far into his mouth. "Why? What for?"

"Something very very important," Drucilla said.

"No."

"We won't take them far," Drucilla assured him. She put her arm around him. Only the night light was on in his room. He had just been tucked in for the night.

"Where?" Courtney still clutched tightly.

"To put in the vehicle," she said gently.

His eyes widened. "To go away?"

"Oh don't be silly. We need them for a game. A journey."

"What journey?"

"Remember how we took our first trip in the vehicle so that we would feel warm and safe in the new house?"

He thought for a minute. "Yes."

"Now we need the vehicle to help us remember where we came from and who we are."

He was sucking his thumb rhythmically and she knew he had no idea of what she meant, but that

was okay. He was flattered to be told and included. He didn't say anything.

"It's a secret project," Drucilla said, backing toward the door. "Think about it. You have till the end of the week."

The next night, at dinner, Mrs. Brattles said, "I thought I had a full set of cake plates and cups and saucers. But one of each is missing."

Mr. Brattles shrugged. "Over the years things break."

"I suppose so. But I always kept track. Some of the silver is missing too. I've looked everywhere."

Drucilla and Esmeralda stared at the tablecloth and then excused themselves.

"What are you two girls up to? You've been working like moles underground in your rooms and in that vehicle. Drucilla, are you scheming again?"

"We're making a surprise," Drucilla said. "A kind of new journey."

"Another surprise? Last time you plotted and planned you turned our lives around. What are you up to now?"

"You'll see."

"When?"

"Saturday."

"The day of the sale."

"It will be a side attraction."

"What a good idea."

Drucilla crossed her fingers under the table.

"Another poster?" Toni said to Drucilla in art class Thursday afternoon. "Can I see?"

"Okay." Drucilla showed her the oak tag sheet.

"Red on white." Toni approved of the colors, but when she read the words she gasped, "Oh Gigi, can you?"

"What do you mean?"

"I mean, can you get away with this? It . . . it's just out-rage-ous."

Drucilla re-read the words on the poster and thought they made perfect sense. "I don't know what you're talking about," she said.

Friday afternoon Courtney presented Drucilla with the bag of animals.

She kissed him on the forehead and let him in to see how they would use the animals in the vehicle. Courtney blinked. "It's like magic," he said, gazing at the transformed interior of the vehicle.

Esmeralda and Drucilla spent the rest of the afternoon arranging the animals and the objects, planning the lighting and the descriptive labels. By Friday night it was done. The selection and arrangement of objects were complete. The chairs had been removed. Everything was in place.

Drucilla and Esmeralda got up very early Saturday morning. They dressed carefully in their oldest, most faded Coves Landing clothes and went downstairs. Neither of them could eat. They took the poster out to the mailbox where it could be propped up so that anyone could see it. They placed it next to their parents' TAG SALE sign. Here is what Drucilla's poster said:

GUIDED TOUR OF
HISTORIC RECREATION OF
BRATTLES-BUNDAGE HOUSEHOLD
VICTIMS OF HARD TIMES.
HELP US SAVE OUR CHERISHED
FAMILY HERITAGE
25 cents

They looked at the sign from different angles and were pleased. Then they went back to the house. Mr. and Mrs. Brattles were coming downstairs for breakfast. Courtney was still asleep.

"My goodness, you're up early," Mrs. Brattles said.

"You can help us set up the tables if you like," said Mr. Brattles.

"We have to work on our project," said Esmeralda.

"The secret surprise in the vehicle?"

"What are you doing anyway?" Mr. Brattles asked.

"An exhibit in the vehicle."

"How sweet," Mrs. Brattles said.

When they had finished their breakfast, Mr. and Mrs. Brattles cleared the table and set to work writing prices on tags and sorting the objects. Then they carried these objects out to the garage where they had set up the Ping-Pong table they had borrowed from the Nolands. "I'm so glad it's a good day," Mrs. Brattles called. "A little nippy, but clear. I think we'll make a nice haul. The ad in the paper and the sign out on the main road were a good idea."

Mr. Brattles arranged ashtrays and candlesticks around a centerpiece of a cut-glass bowl. Mrs. Brattles hung the contents of the trunks on a clothes rack she had rented for the occasion. There were several of the smocked dresses and a few women's clothes including the heather tweed "good wool." Mrs. Brattles looked at the dress and shuddered. "Years of torture itching in that thing, over at last. Even the moths wouldn't take it." She turned to Drucilla and gave her a searching look. "Drucilla, is there anything you would like to sell today?"

"I don't have a thing to sell," Drucilla said desperately.

"Nothing?"

"Nothing."

"Very well. Help me set these dresses up and put the shoes neatly in pairs beneath the rack."

Then the first cars pulled in. "Come have a look at our things," Mrs. Brattles called to the grinning man behind the wheel.

"We're here for the guided tour."

"This way," Drucilla beckoned from the front door. The man, his wife and two children (one of whom was in Esmeralda's class) followed her into the house.

"The guided what?" Mrs. Brattles said. Another car pulled in and two people got out. One of them headed for the house, the other to look at the table full of objects. Drucilla stood at the front door and panicked. What would she say? She stared at the driveway. There on the tables and racks of their garage and driveway were all the little objects that she had known since her life began. Pin cushions, stocking bags, chipped mugs, dessert plates, napkin rings etched with the initials of family long gone. Photographs and portraits in tarnished frames. Little things, but they had made up the safe corners of her world and now they sat out in the fall sunlight like refuse. She remembered what she had to say. "Step this way, my sister will take the fee."

Esmeralda collected the twenty-five cents each and led them into the foyer. Then with great ceremony she drew the blanket aside to reveal the interior of the vehicle. Within the vehicle, Drucilla and Esmeralda had created a miniature world. Using the animals as its inhabitants, and a velvet bedspread as a background, they had set out the carefully selected objects (all labeled) to create a small facsimile of the world they had known at Coves Landing. On the velvet Drucilla had pinned her locket, as well as Esmeralda's baby bracelet and two miniature portraits in which those pieces of jewelry had been painted. There was a silver-plate candlestick and the découpage toy chest, a baby's rocker and a painting of grapes on velvet. There were selections of china and a water goblet. There were photographs of the game room and the veranda.

Drucilla began hesitantly. "The dresses my sister and I are wearing are original models from Best and Company, in New York. My granny always ordered them. I think they are from nineteen forty-four. They are made of a hundred-percent cotton and belonged to my Aunt Delphi Bloomer. She saved them in a trunk and they were worn by my cousin Blakesly and then by me and Esmeralda. On your left is a candlestick—" She stopped to catch her breath. "Now, that candlestick was bought in Boston by

my father's great-uncle. He bought it because he told his wife he was going to Boston for the day, but he went to a party and got sick," Drucilla sighed, "and had to stay overnight. He bought the candlestick so his wife wouldn't be mad at him. He told her it was silver. But then she found out it's only plate." This tale drew a few chuckles and Drucilla began to enjoy giving guided tours. "Over here is a découpage toy chest made by an ancestor of ours. Her name was Muffin Egli. Well now"—Drucilla took a deep breath—"there are plenty of stories about her, but I'll only tell you that she made that chest after her father broke up her romance with a sailor and she threatened to run away and follow him and her father locked her in the house and she made that chest. Later she did get married, but she never used the chest for toys. She kept her spare linen in it."

"There's a group waiting outside," said Esmeralda.

"Tell them it will be a few more minutes," Drucilla said.

Drucilla did three tours and each time she got better. She told family stories. She made people laugh. At the end of each tour she said, "The contribution you make will help our family out so we won't have to sell our things. Please don't buy any of the items you see for sale outside," she concluded with a wave toward the door. "We love them and want to keep them for ourselves and for those who will follow us."

Chrissy was in Drucilla's second tour and Chipper Mallory and his mother turned up in the third.

"What are you doing here, Chipper?" Drucilla said.

"Want to take the tour," he said, swaying from foot to foot.

"What if I won't let you?"

"Aw come on, Gigi."

"From now on call me Drucilla," she said icily.

"What?" He stopped swaying.

"You heard me, Charles."

At the end of the fifth tour Mr. and Mrs. Brattles suddenly appeared at the door. "Don't stop, Drucilla," Mr. Brattle said. "It's beginning to rain and so we're canceling our sale."

Esmeralda slipped out the door without a word to bring in their poster.

Drucilla cut the tour short. "I suppose that's it," she said. Then she blew out the candles and ushered her group to the front door. With Esmeralda she helped her parents bring the objects in out of the cold drizzle. As they passed each other in the door, Esmeralda said, "Hey Drucie, we won."

"Shhhh," Drucilla hissed. She saw her mother's dejected figure out in the driveway, gathering together the unsold items. "We won, but they lost."

"It's so chilly," Mrs. Brattles said to her husband. She set down the last load of things and looked around the kitchen, rubbing her hands together. "I'll make a hot lunch."

"Can I help?" Drucilla said.

"No," Mrs. Brattles answered quickly, not looking at her.

"Go inside, Drucilla," Mr. Brattles said. "Your mother and I have things to discuss." His face was pale and his voice flat. "Esme, go upstairs and wash Courtney for lunch."

Drucilla stood in the middle of the living room as she had on the first day they had moved into the house. She realized that she had gotten the wish she had made that day. The room was like the one in the carpet advertisement. They could arrange themselves on the wall-to-wall in their new bright clothes and smile, and you wouldn't know them from the picture. But on that first day when the house had been awful they had been a family, depending upon one another, and giving comfort to one another. Now the house was warm and sound but the drear and gloom of that first day had not disappeared—it was worse. Drucilla knew her parents were hurt and disappointed. The success of her own plan made her miserable. She couldn't tell them about it. She couldn't share it with them. Three months ago they had shared each other's hopes and good news.

"Lunch is ready," Mrs. Brattles called. Esmeralda and Courtney came downstairs.

When they all sat down, Drucilla stared across the table at her mother's long discouraged face. She could not eat a thing.

"Well then," Mrs. Brattles sighed. "I wonder what we did wrong."

"You had good publicity," Esmeralda piped; "maybe it was the weather."

"We weren't talking about the sale," Mr. Brattles said, "but about how we raised you girls."

"Us?" Esmeralda said, growing pale as her father.

Mr. Brattles nodded. "We thought we had raised you to be honest and forthright with us and to know the difference between a surprise and deceit. Drucilla," he turned to her, "since you are so interested in your heritage, you should know that it includes honesty as well as determination."

The lump that had prevented Drucilla from swallowing food now seemed to rise so that her eyes smarted and the thing she hated most to do was going to happen. She would cry in front of Esme and Courtney.

Mrs. Brattles reached across the table and covered Drucilla's hand with her own. "Winston," she said softly. "Perhaps we should show the children that part of our heritage is also good grace and the ability to bury anger and disappointment."

After a moment Mr. Brattles nodded. "Good grace," he repeated. "Incidentally Drucilla, Muffin Egli married the sailor." He paused to let his words sink in. "The very same sailor she wanted to follow in the first place."

"I didn't know that," Drucilla said.

"Many people didn't. Muffin and her father didn't tell. Muffin was a determined girl. She got her way, but she had the good grace not to rub her father's nose in her victory. Muffin taught her father something, but he had taught her something to begin with. They had learned from each other."

"I didn't know any of that," Drucilla said in a whisper. All at once she realized that her parents knew the truth about her tour. That was why they had been angry. They knew everything. What a relief.

Relief made her very hungry.

"You certainly put that vehicle of yours to good use, girls," Mrs. Brattles said after a pause. "You did a fine job with it."

Mr. Brattles agreed. Then he tilted his head back and laughed and the pink light came into his face and it seemed to Drucilla that the house and room turned warm and pleasant reflecting that light. "I must confess," he said. "Your mother and I managed to get carried away without any vehicle at all. Didn't we, Cordy?"

Mrs. Brattles smiled and nodded. "We even went too far."

Drucilla looked through the door of the kitchen into the foyer at the vehicle. The blankets were soiled and it had begun to tilt dangerously to one side. "I think we ought to take it down," she said.

"No," Courtney wailed, "what about the journey?"

"It's over," Drucilla said.

The vehicle had taken them from an unknown dismal house full of worry, to this place of comfort and trust. "We don't need to go anywhere now," Drucilla said. "We're there."

THE EGYPTOLOGY HANDBOOK
A COURSE IN THE WONDERS OF EGYPT
MISS EMILY SANDS
INVITES YOU TO DISCOVER
THE TREASURES OF
ANCIENT EGYPT
SPECIAL TICKET
ADMIT ONE
ACCESS UNLIMITED

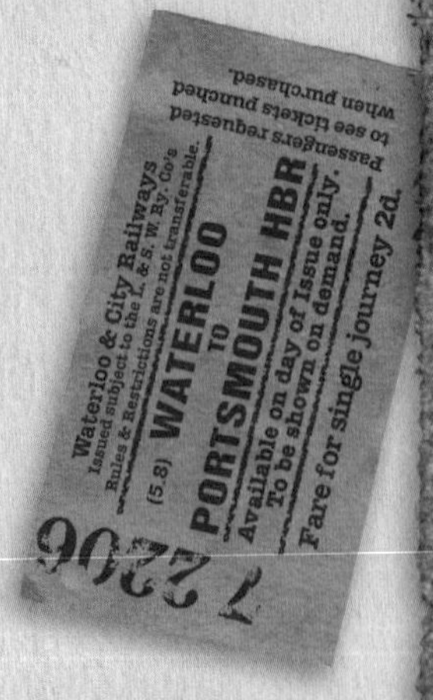


*The Sphinx, left, stands guard over the Giza Plateau. A colossal statue with the body of a lion and the head of a man, it has been twice buried and twice rescued from the shifting sands. Around 1490 BC, it was uncovered by the royal prince who was to become King Thutmosis IV, and in AD 1925, it was uncovered again by French engineer Emile Baraize.*

Waterloo & City Railways
Issued subject to the L. & S. W. Ry. Co's
(8.1) DORKING
TO
LONDON WATERLOO
To be shown on demand and
given up on return journey.
Fare for double journey 3d.
Passengers requested to see tickets punched when purchased.
E 4294

Walk Like an Egyptian!
On a Rambling Rameses Walking Tour of Egypt
Available November – February, From Cairo to Luxor and Back.


Designed by Jonathan Lambert and Nghiem Ta

First U.S. edition 2005
Library of Congress Catalog Number is available.
ISBN 0-7636-2932-4
4 6 8 10 9 7 5 3
Manufactured in China
Candlewick Press
2067 Massachusetts Avenue, Cambridge, Massachusetts 02140
visit us at www.candlewick.com

Publisher's note: According to the editors, LIZ FLANAGAN and DUGALD STEER, when the publisher received the manuscript of Egyptology: Search for the Tomb of Osiris from Joanna Sutherland in 2004, it was thought that no further works by Miss Emily Sands, who went missing on an expedition up the Nile in 1927, would be forthcoming. But it now appears that one of the detectives hired by Lady Farncombe to investigate the Sands disappearance may actually have uncovered another book, which Emily had been preparing for her niece and nephew. However, since the publisher still cannot say for certain that a Miss Sands ever existed, readers must decide for themselves whether the story is true or simply an elaborate concoction.

www.egyptology1926.com

*One of the Colossi of Memnon, West Bank, Luxor*
*Built around 1360 BC by King Amenhotep III*

# The Egyptology Handbook

## PART I: THE HISTORY OF ANCIENT EGYPT



## PART II: LIFE AND CULTURE IN ANCIENT EGYPT



## PART III: GODS AND RELIGION IN ANCIENT EGYPT



## APPENDICES

*This photograph shows the members of my "Egyptology" expedition standing in front of the pyramids.*

*A photograph of the temple of the crocodile god, Sobek, at Kom Ombo*

*You can add these Egyptian stamps to your collection.*

The "Bennu Bird"
27th December 1926

My Dearest Niece and Nephew,

I am very sorry that I will not be able to come and see you during the Christmas holidays. I do so look forward to the lovely time we spend together each year. As you know from the postcard which I sent from Luxor, I am having an exciting time leading an expedition that is going up the River Nile in Egypt, looking for a lost tomb. I am travelling on an old-fashioned sailing barge called the "Bennu Bird." Although we spend most mornings visiting ancient tombs and temples, I still have quite a lot of time on my hands. So as well as writing a journal of my expedition, I have written a book to teach you all about Ancient Egypt.

I expect that I shall be in Egypt until March or April — but if all goes well, it could be longer. I must stop writing now because my boat is just about to dock at Edfu, near the famous Temple of Horus. Do say a big "Hello" to Lady Amanda for me, if you see her, and to Mummy and Daddy, too. Let them know I shall send a card as soon as I have more news!

Your Loving Aunt,

Emily

Giza Plateau
Memphis
Saqqara
River Nile
The Red Sea
Beni Hasan
Akhetaten
Abydos
Valley of the Kings
Deir El Bahri
Thebes
Edfu
Great Western Desert
Elephantine
Philae
Abu Simbel
N
NW
NE
W
E
SW
SE
S
Hypostyle Hall, Karnak
Temple of Rameses ll, Abu Simbel

*Part I*

# The History of Ancient Egypt

Nearly five thousand years ago, the lands that lay along the northernmost part of the River Nile were united for the first time under a single king known as Narmer. Believed by his people to be a living god, Narmer was the first of many hundreds of pharaohs under whose rule the land of Egypt became home to one of the most impressive civilisations the world has ever known. As you can see in the Chronology of Egyptian History on pages 74 and 75, it was a culture that would last in a substantially similar form for more than three thousand years.

Obelisk of Thutmosis I

*Concerning Egypt itself I shall extend my remarks to a great length, because there is no other country that possesses so many wonders, nor any that has such a number of works that defy description.*
*"The Histories," Herodotus, 440 BC*

## Lesson 1

# The Origins of Egypt: Up to 2650 BC

Egypt was home to people thousands of years before the pharaohs. Archaeologists have found traces of these people, who settled into communities along the banks of the River Nile. Their fine pottery, jewellery, and flint tools show us how skilled they were. These people began farming and domesticating animals. They also began to wage war as they fought for control of this fertile strip of land on either side of the great river.

*According to some historical sources, around the year 2900 BC, Narmer, a king from Hieraconpolis, unified Upper Egypt, the part of Egypt that lies south of modern Cairo, with Lower Egypt, the area north of Cairo, including the Nile Delta. The first historical king of Egypt, Narmer founded the first of more than thirty dynasties of Egyptian kings.*

*Right: This palette shows King Narmer defeating an enemy. Some people believe that it commemorates the unification of Egypt.*

*Left: A golden hawk's head from Hieraconpolis*

## LEGENDARY ORIGINS

The Ancient Egyptians themselves believed that the king who united Egypt and founded its capital at Memphis was called Menes. Whether Menes was the same person as Narmer or a legend created from stories about several kings, no one knows.

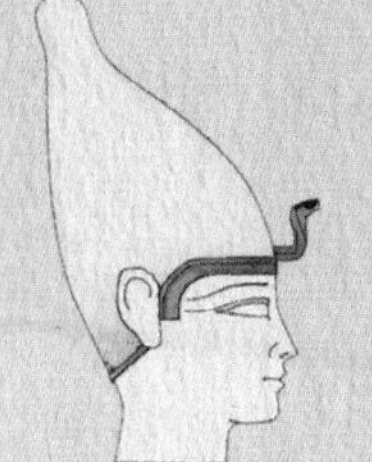

White Crown

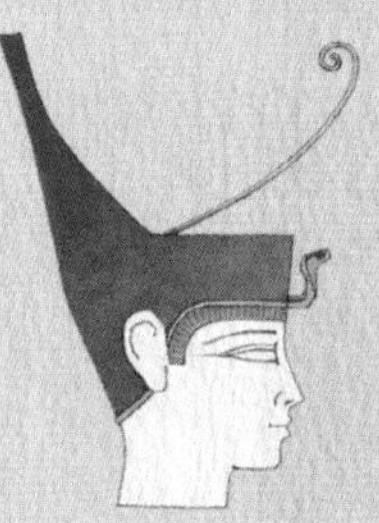

Red Crown

*From earliest times, the king of Egypt wore a crown that symbolised his rule over the two parts of Egypt. This double crown was made by joining the traditional white crown of Upper Egypt to the red crown of Lower Egypt.*

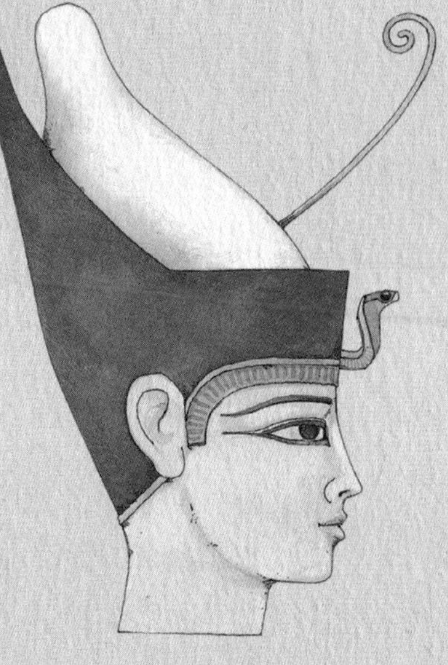

Double Crown

ACTIVITY: You can see from the chronology on pages 74–75 that Ancient Egyptian history is divided into three main periods: the Old Kingdom, the Middle Kingdom, and the New Kingdom. Here are the names of some important Old Kingdom kings, along with the dates they ruled. Can you put them in order, oldest first?

Khaefra 2520–2494 BC
Snefru 2575–2551 BC
Djedefra 2528–2520 BC
Menkaura 2490–2472 BC
Khufu 2551–2528 BC

ANSWERS: Snefru, Khufu, Djedefra, Khaefra, Menkaura

## Lesson 2

# The Old Kingdom: 2650 to 2450 BC

The kings of Egypt's first royal dynasties were very powerful. Treated as a living god, the king was seen as the only person who could speak to the gods and ensure peace and stability throughout the land. To understand the strength and influence of these Old Kingdom kings, you have only to look at their greatest legacy, which still dominates the Egyptian landscape: the pyramids. The famous pyramids at Giza didn't spring from the imagination of an Egyptian architect perfectly formed. Instead, there were several stages of development as various kings experimented with different styles of tombs.

*The Old Kingdom pharaoh King Menkaura and his wife, Queen Khamerernebty*

*The illustrations below show the rise and fall in the height of the pyramids. King Snefru was the most prolific builder. He had three pyramids constructed – two based on a stepped design and a third "true" pyramid.*

*Step Pyramid of Zoser, 2630 BC 204 ft. (62 m.)*

*Pyramid of Meidum, Snefru, 2600 BC 306 ft. (92 m.)*

*Bent Pyramid, Snefru, 2600 BC 344 ft. (105 m.)*

*Red Pyramid, Snefru, 2600 BC 341 ft. (104 m.)*

## SAQQARA

At Saqqara, to the west of the new city of Memphis, the kings and nobles built their enormous tombs. It was there that King Zoser commissioned his royal architect Imhotep to build the world's first monumental stone building — the Step Pyramid.

*King Zoser's Step Pyramid was surrounded by a large wall that enclosed temples and courtyards.*

1. *Step Pyramid*
2. *Courtyard*
3. *Sed Festival court*
4. *Storerooms*
5. *Funerary temple & pyramid entrance*
6. *North court*

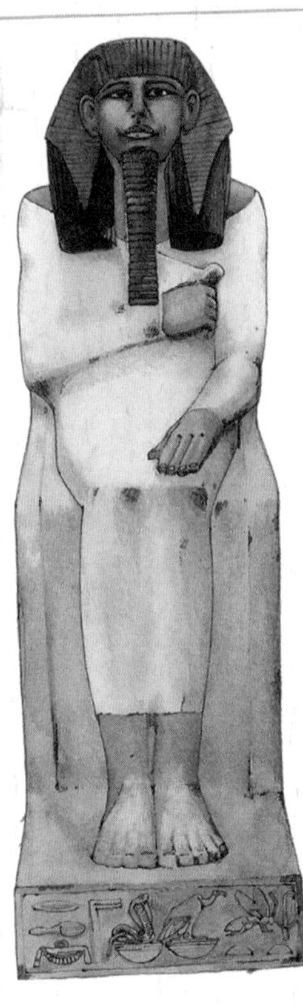

*In 1924, a life-size statue of King Zoser was discovered at Saqqara by Cecil Firth. Wearing a Sed cloak, worn by the king during his jubilee Sed Festival, the statue would have been given offerings on behalf of the dead king.*

## KING ZOSER'S BURIAL CHAMBER

The burial chamber was located underneath the Step Pyramid, surrounded by a maze of passages decorated with carvings and hieroglyphs recording the king's name.

## Lesson 4

# The Great Pyramids

The magnificent pyramids at Giza are the most famous of all Ancient Egyptian monuments. Each pyramid was part of a larger burial complex that included a valley temple, to which the king's body was brought by boat; a connecting causeway, along which the funeral procession would bring the body; and a mortuary temple for the burial ceremonies.

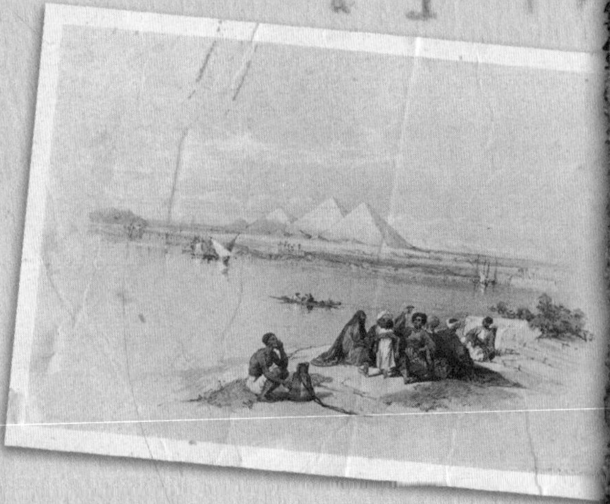

THE PYRAMIDS AT GIZA IN CROSS SECTION

The pyramids of Khufu, Khaefra, and Menkaura were broken into by tomb robbers long ago. Apart from the stone sarcophagi found inside, they are all now empty. They were built from limestone, with granite burial chambers and fine limestone outer casings.

The Great Pyramid of Khufu

The Pyramid of Khaefra

The Pyramid of Menkaura

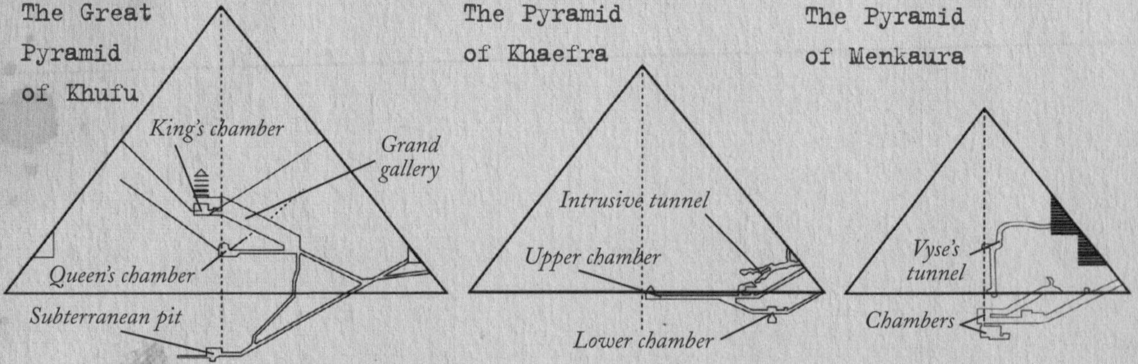


*With their fine white limestone outer casings, the pyramids must have looked even more magnificent in antiquity. Sadly, most of the outer casings were removed and used to rebuild the city of Cairo after an earthquake.*

HOW WERE THE PYRAMIDS BUILT?

No one is sure how the pyramids were built. More than two million blocks were used for the Great Pyramid alone, each one weighing about two and a half tons. Here are three theories, each with its own advantages and drawbacks:

THEORY 1: Earth Ramps

Stones would have been dragged up huge ramps of earth and put in place. But such ramps would need vast amounts of earth to build.

THEORY 2: Pulleys or Cranes

Enormous pulleys would have been built to hoist each stone into place. But these pulleys would need to be incredibly strong and tall to reach the top of the pyramid.

THEORY 3: Spiral Causeway

Pathways of mud brick would have been coiled around the edge of the pyramid and the stones pulled up on sledges. But no evidence of mud brick pathways has been found.

ACTIVITY: There are some very strange theories as to how the pyramids were built. What is the strangest theory you can find?

*Lesson 5*

# The Middle Kingdom: 2040 to 1750 BC

At the end of the Old Kingdom, Ancient Egypt entered a time now known as the First Intermediate Period. The ordered life of the Old Kingdom was swept away as tradition and central government under a single king broke down. When order was eventually reestablished by the pharaohs of the Middle Kingdom, Ancient Egyptian society had begun to look a little different.

*The Middle Kingdom kings came from Thebes and brought their local god, Amun (pictured below), with them when they rose to power. Soon he was worshipped throughout Egypt as king of the gods.*

*Although the kings were still seen as godlike, ordinary people had begun to enjoy more privilege and so the wealthy also started to create lavish tombs. The painting above shows one of those tombs at Beni Hasan, cut into the face of the rock.*

## TOMB RAIDERS

To achieve safe passage to the afterlife, it was essential that the mummified body and its precious belongings remain undisturbed. Tomb builders devised many clever defences against tomb robbers, such as false doors and secret passageways, but sadly many of them failed. So many tombs now being excavated lie empty, with only a few tantalising fragments left behind.

ACTIVITY: After an archaeological dig, you discover that the labels have come off your valuable finds. Can you correctly identify these objects and give each one the right label?

1.

2.

3.

4.

*A. A brain hook was used to remove the brain before mummification.*

*B. Canopic jars were used to store the internal organs of the deceased.*

*C. A throw stick was a weapon that was used for hunting birds.*

*D. This bracelet once belonged to an Egyptian queen called Ahotep.*

ANSWERS: 1-B; 2-A; 3-D; 4-C

## Lesson 6

# Pyramid Texts and Tombs

The Ancient Egyptians believed that writing contained great power. From the time of the pharaoh Unas at the end of the Old Kingdom and right through the Middle Kingdom, the walls of the royal burial chambers were covered in hieroglyphs. These Pyramid Texts were spells and magical incantations to be used by the dead king to help him in his journey to the afterlife.

*According to the Ancient Egyptians, if a dead person's name was spoken, he or she would live again, so many tombs show the occupant's name repeated over and over. Can you find the name Pepi on this fragment from his tomb, at left?*

= P P

= I I

COFFIN TEXTS

During the Middle Kingdom, rich people were buried in wooden coffins decorated with brightly coloured writing. Like the royal Pyramid Texts, these Coffin Texts contained potent magic to protect the dead person and ensure well-being in the afterlife.

*Ancient Egyptian Coffin*

## THE AFTERLIFE

Ancient Egyptians believed that what was shown on the walls of their tombs would also exist in the afterlife. They were careful to depict, either as paintings or models, whatever they required for a comfortable existence after death, whether it was food, servants, or music to last for eternity.

ACTIVITY: These pictures come from the tomb walls of a rich Egyptian named Ti, Overseer of Royal Mortuary Structures. What activities did he wish to enjoy in the afterlife?

*1.*

*2.*

*3.*

Draw some tomb pictures of your own life. You could even try adding your name in hieroglyphs (See pages 50–51 for help).

ANSWERS: 1. Building boats 2. Hunting hippos 3. Herding cranes

# Lesson 7
# An Ancient Egyptian Tale

This Middle Kingdom tale, THE STORY OF THE SHIPWRECKED SAILOR, was written by Amenaa, son of Ameny, the cunning-fingered scribe. May he live long in health and wealth!

I was on my way to the pharaoh's mines on a fine ship, in the company of one hundred and fifty of Egypt's best sailors. As we approached land, the winds picked up and the waves grew high and soon our ship was lost. I managed to seize a piece of wood to save myself, but all the other sailors were drowned.

The waves washed me ashore on a deserted island, but luckily I found plenty of food - figs, melons, fish, and fowl - and I lacked for nothing. And so I lit a fire and made an offering to the gods. All of a sudden there was a noise like thunder; the trees shook and the ground trembled and I saw a huge serpent!

It was mighty, blue as lapis lazuli and all overlaid with gold. It drew itself up before me as I cowered on the ground, and three times it asked me, "What has brought you here, little one? If you don't tell me, I will make you vanish just like a flame." And it carried me away in its mouth.

I told the serpent about my voyage and the shipwreck. And it said to me, "Fear not. If you have come to me, it is the gods who let you live and brought you here to this blessed isle." And it said that I would remain on its island for four months, until a ship came bearing sailors from my own land to take me home to my wife and children.

The serpent seemed to enjoy company and conversation, and it talked at length with me. It told me how it lived on the island of plenty with its kindred, and how there were 75 serpents altogether.

I bowed and told it that it would be rewarded by the pharaoh, with gifts of perfume, oil, and ships laden with treasures. But it just smiled and said, "I am the Prince of Punt and I already have such riches. When you depart from my island, you will never see it again, for it will be changed into waves."

Time went by, and, just as the serpent had said, after four months had passed, one day I saw a ship. I climbed up a tree so I could see who was aboard, and then rushed to tell the serpent. It already knew all about it, and said, "Farewell, farewell. Go home, little one. Within two months you will be at your house once more. Embrace your children and may your name be blessed amongst your people."

I bowed and thanked the serpent, and it gave me parting gifts of perfume, sweet wood, kohl, incense, and ivory. I went down to the shore and met the sailors, who took me aboard their ship.

Just as the serpent had said, after two months we arrived home again, and I sought out the pharaoh's courtiers and before the whole court I presented the pharaoh with the serpent's gifts and my story was heard.

ACTIVITY: This is one of the most famous Ancient Egyptian tales. Another is THE STORY OF SINUHE. See if you can find it in your local library.

# The New Kingdom: 1550 to 1070 BC

After the Middle Kingdom, Egypt was ruled by foreigners known as the Hyksos kings, who introduced the horse, the chariot, and new bronze weapons. These weapons would prove very useful to the warrior-kings who dominated the New Kingdom. These kings were determined to make Egypt as strong as possible and waged war against their neighbours, creating the most powerful empire of the ancient world.

*Rameses II in His War Chariot*

THE FEMALE PHARAOH

Not all of the New Kingdom kings were warlike. When Pharaoh Thutmosis II died, his widow, Hatshepsut, acted first as regent for her nephew Thutmosis III and for 15 years ruled as pharaoh alone.

*Hatshepsut's mortuary temple, below, was built into the rock near the Valley of the Kings and is still an impressive sight.*

*Hatshepsut, above, wasn't the only female pharaoh. All adopted the symbolic artificial beard of the pharaoh.*

## AFTER THE NEW KINGDOM — ALEXANDER

When the New Kingdom ended, Ancient Egypt again fell under the sway of foreign rulers. The Persians, who ruled Egypt until 332 BC, were so unpopular that when the Greek emperor Alexander the Great defeated them, he was greeted as a liberator. He founded the city of Alexandria, which became renowned as a centre of culture and learning based around its famous museum and library.

*The Temple of Horus at Edfu was rebuilt by Alexander's successor, Ptolemy I, who founded a new dynasty of Greek pharaohs.*

## CLEOPATRA

Queen Cleopatra VII is one of the most famous figures in Ancient Egyptian history. She inherited the throne at a time when the Roman Empire was closing in on Egypt. Intelligent and ambitious, she had affairs with both Julius Caesar and Mark Antony. After Antony's defeat, she is said to have killed herself rather than be humiliated by Rome. Her death marks the end of Ancient Egypt.

ACTIVITY: Design a coin commemorating Cleopatra's reign, with her head on one side and an event from her life on the other.

## Lesson 9

# The Valley of the Kings

The tombs of the New Kingdom pharaohs lie across the Nile from Luxor, in the Valley of the Kings. Most of these tombs were plundered in antiquity, their treasures taken and the royal mummies reburied in groups. But Howard Carter, the famous Egyptologist, was convinced that one tomb had escaped discovery. He spent years searching and digging until, in 1922, he finally uncovered a mysterious flight of stone steps leading to a tomb entrance.

*Making a hole in the tomb door, Carter looked into the antechamber. He was amazed to see that the contents were almost intact and that there were "animals, statues, and gold — everywhere the glint of gold."*

*This solid gold mummy mask is made in the image of King Tutankhamen.*

Tutankhamen's outer two coffins were plated in gold.

INSIDE THE TOMB

The contents of Tutankhamen's tomb told a story: Long ago, robbers had begun a raid but were interrupted, scattering treasures on the floor as they escaped. All was jumbled together: linen, jewel boxes, gold rings, and perfumes. But at the heart of the tomb, in his burial chamber, King Tutankhamen lay undisturbed in his cocoon of three coffins.

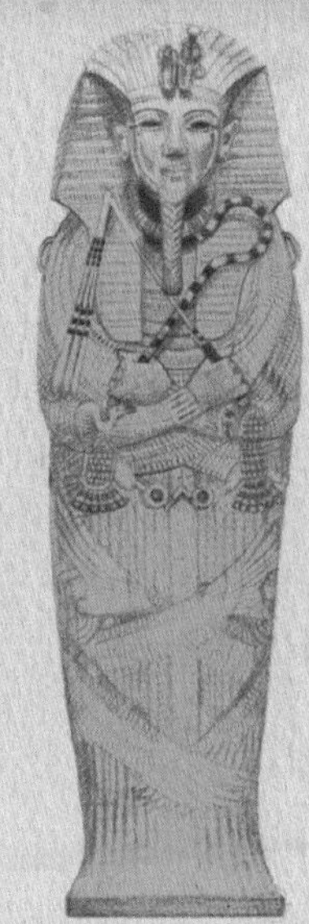

The inner coffin was made of 240 pounds of solid gold.

A "Mummy's Curse" is said to protect the tombs of the pharaohs. Lord Carnarvon's death shortly after the opening of Tutankhamen's tomb was supposedly evidence of this curse in action. But at least as I write this, in 1926, Howard Carter and his assistants seem to have escaped it....

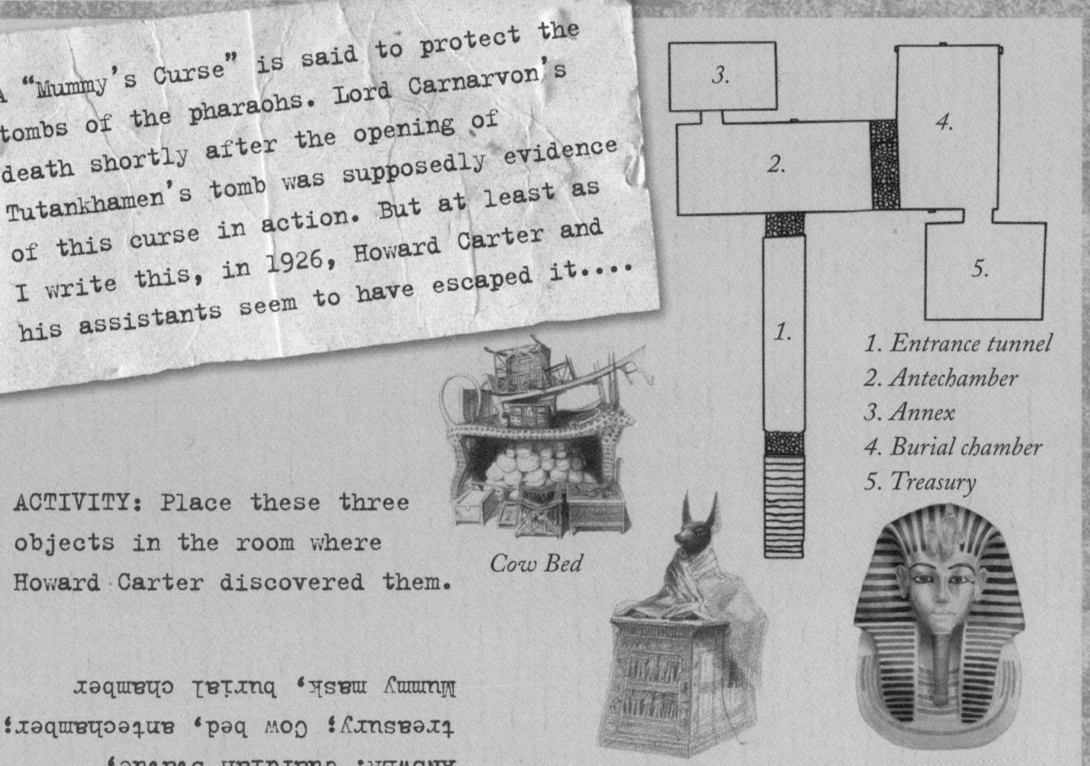


Cow Bed

Guardian Statue

Mummy Mask

ACTIVITY: Place these three objects in the room where Howard Carter discovered them.

ANSWER: Guardian statue, treasury; Cow bed, antechamber; Mummy mask, burial chamber

*This map shows some of the resources of Ancient Egypt. Ancient Egyptians also imported many things: wood from Lebanon, ivory from Assyria, olive oil from Crete, and incense from Punt.*

## Part II
# Life and Culture in Ancient Egypt

*The gentle man overcomes all obstacles. He who makes himself work all day will never know a moment of enjoyment, but he who spends all day enjoying himself will not be able to hold on to his wealth.*
*"The Wisdom of Ptah-hotep," c. 1900 BC*

The history of Ancient Egypt is not merely the history of kings and queens. For many thousands of years, the culture that grew up along the banks of the Nile was one of the most civilised in the ancient world. Ancient Egypt was rich in resources, and those that it lacked, such as wood or olive oil, it was able to import from its neighbours. This allowed civilised culture to develop.

In some villages that have been excavated, such as Deir El Medina on the West Bank at Luxor, there is evidence that a large number of the population could read and write, including a number of women.

# Lesson 10
# Life on the Flooding Nile

The rhythms of the River Nile defined many aspects of Ancient Egyptian life. Every year the river had a season of flooding, when the water would rise to cover the farmland. When it receded once more, the fields would be left covered in a layer of fertile black silt. But if the Nile rose too high, it might cause damage, sweeping away people's homes. And if the water levels weren't high enough, the whole country would suffer from the famine that resulted from a bad harvest.

*The Ancient Egyptians called Egypt "Kemet," or the "black land," while the vast desert area that lay beyond the black fertile strip was called "Desheret," or the "red land."*

*The god of the flooding Nile is Hapi, shown here. His plump appearance represents the plentiful bounty of the river.*

THE "BENNU BIRD"

The Ancient Egyptians were great boat-builders. Our hired sailing barge — or "dahabeeyah" — the "Bennu Bird," is the modern descendant of those ancient boats.

*Much mythology is tied up with the Nile. This scene, right, from the walls of the temple at Edfu shows Horus fighting his enemy Seth, who has taken on the form of a hippo.*

ACTIVITY: The Ancient Egyptians would undertake some tasks when the river was in flood and others when the flood had receded. Decide which of these activities are best done when the Nile is in flood and which when it is out of flood.

*Building Pyramids*

*Planting Seeds*

*Harvesting Crops*

*Going to War*

ANSWER: It is best to build pyramids and go to war during the flood season, as you cannot farm the land then, but planting and harvesting crops must be done before the flood returns.

## Lesson 11

# Eat Like an Egyptian

Rich Ancient Egyptians loved to entertain and would have served up feasts including such delicacies as pigeon stew, roast quail, spiced honey cakes, and fresh berries. Although not everyone could eat as well as this, it is certain that many people would have enjoyed a wide variety of such foods as meat, fish, eggs, cheese, grapes, figs, melons, onions, garlic, leeks, and lettuce.

DAILY BREAD

For ordinary Ancient Egyptians, bread was the most important food. Sometimes workers were paid in grain. Grinding the barley or emmer wheat to make each day's flour was a hard job usually done by women.

EASY FISH

The Nile was full of fish, and when the flood receded, some were left high and dry on the banks. They could be grilled straightaway or preserved by drying or pickling in salt.

HUNTING FOR FOOD

While some pharaohs enjoyed elephant-hunting expeditions, it was more common to hunt animals that could be eaten, such as hares, antelope, gazelles, and different kinds of waterfowl and birds.

BEER

Most Ancient Egyptians drank beer. This was because beer was often healthier to drink than unclean water from the Nile, which might well have carried disease. Wine was also available for rich people.

ACTIVITY: Try making this Ancient Egyptian recipe.

HUMMUS

12 oz. (300 gr.) cooked chickpeas
juice of 1 lemon
2 cloves garlic
sesame seed oil
1/2 tsp salt

Mash up the cooked chickpeas, then add the lemon juice, chopped garlic, and as much sesame seed oil as it takes to make a paste smooth enough to spread on bread. This tasty dish is as popular today as it was thousands of years ago.

## Lesson 12

# Dress Like an Egyptian

Ancient Egyptians took great care with their appearance. Most clothing was made of linen and varied from simple shifts to richly decorated, pleated robes. Wealthy people shaved their heads and wore elaborately styled wigs to protect themselves from the hot sun and guard against lice. Children had a hairstyle that would seem strange to us today: both boys and girls had their hair shaved off, except for a lock hanging down by the ear.

*Ancient Egyptians used perfumed oils to clean, protect, and scent their skin. A jar of perfumed oil was found in the tomb of Tutankhamen as part of his equipment for the afterlife.*

*At parties and special occasions, a host might offer guests perfumed cones of wax to place on their heads. As they heated up, the cones would melt and slowly drip down the guests' hair and faces!*

MAKEUP

Both men and women wore eye makeup known as kohl, which also protected against the strong glare of the sun. It was ground to a paste on a palette and then carefully applied with the help of a mirror.

JEWELLERY

The Ancient Egyptians loved jewellery. Metals and stones were worked into exquisite bracelets, earrings, necklaces, and rings of gold, lapis lazuli, amethyst, turquoise, and precious stones.

*Left: A statue of Queen Nefertiti*
*Below: Bracelets of King Djer*

ACTIVITY: Working at a dig, you've uncovered these objects. What are they?

ANSWERS: 1. A comb 2. A mirror 3. Perfume jars 4. A bracelet

Lesson 13

# An Egyptian Village

When the New Kingdom kings began building tombs in the Valley of the Kings, they needed workmen nearby. A village of craftspeople was set up at Deir El Medina. When excavated, it gave fascinating insights into the lives of ordinary Egyptians. Remains of letters and lists written by the workers were found there. Reading over these fragments — from laundry lists to evidence in court cases — we can catch glimpses of the concerns of real people thousands of years ago.

A HOUSE PLAN

Deir El Medina was surrounded by a wall, with one entrance to the north. There was a main street and about 70 narrow houses, all constructed in a similar design.

1. Entrance hall
2. Main room
3. Kitchen
4. Storage room or cellar
5. Stairs to open roof area

*This plan shows the cross section of a typical house in Deir El Medina. These houses were designed to stay as cool as possible.*

LETTERS FROM DEIR EL MEDINA

The people living at Deir El Medina were highly skilled and included carpenters, sculptors, and coppersmiths, as well as doctors, scribes, and the officials who oversaw the workers. Scholars disagree as to how many of these people could write themselves and how many would have asked scribes to write for them. People wrote on papyrus and also on thin limestone pieces called ostraca.

ACTIVITY: When these ostraca were first excavated, some had fallen to pieces and had to be reconstructed. They are shown translated here. Can you fit the pieces together?

*A.*

I AM A FREE WOMAN OF EGYP
CHILDREN AND HAVE PROVIDE
SUITABLE TO THEIR STATION IN
GROWN OLD AND BEHOLD, M
AFTER ME ANY MORE. I WILL T
THE ONES WHO HAVE TAKEN C
ANYTHING TO THE ONES WHO

*B.*

MENTMOSE PROMISED HIM
BARLEY FROM MY BROTHER.
THIS TRANSACTION. MAY RI
ON THAT DAY THE WORKMA
FRESH FAT TO THE CHIEF OF

*C.*

HE SAYS: HEAR MY VOICE, D
DO NOT UNTIE YOUR HEAR
DO NOT LET YOUR HEART
PRAISE THE KING, MAY YOU

*D.*

. I HAVE RAISED EIGHT
D THEM WITH EVERYTHING
LIFE. BUT NOW I HAVE
Y CHILDREN DON'T LOOK
HEREFORE GIVE MY GOODS TO
ARE OF ME. I WILL NOT GIVE
HAVE NEGLECTED ME.

*E.*

'I WILL PAY YOU FOR IT WITH
MY BROTHER WILL GUARANTEE
E KEEP YOU IN GOOD HEALTH.'
AN MENNA GAVE A POT OF
POLICE MENTMOSE.

*F.*

DO NOT AVOID MY WORDS,
T FROM WHAT I TELL YOU.
STRAY FROM GOD.
U LOVE HIM, AS A WORKER.

ANSWERS: A & D, from "The Will of Lady Naunakhte"
B & E, from "The Trial of Mentmose"
C & F, from "The Teaching Made by a Man for His Son"

## Lesson 14

# Jobs and Work in Ancient Egypt

Many jobs in Ancient Egypt would have been similar to ones we know today. People worked as farmers, soldiers, midwives, butchers, carpenters, and so on. Other professions were linked to Ancient Egypt's particular traditions — embalmers and temple priests, for example — or were connected to the government or king, like the vizier, the palace dancers, and the pharaoh's royal fan-bearer.

*Anubis was the patron god of embalmers and healers.*

ACTIVITY: Match these tomb inscriptions to the following professions: draughtsman, soldier, doctor.

*A.*
ONE WHO UNDERSTANDS THE INTERNAL FLUIDS AND WHO IS GUARDIAN OF THE BODY.
CURE FOR INDIGESTION:
CRUSH A BOAR'S TOOTH AND PUT IT INSIDE FOUR HONEY CAKES. EAT FOR FOUR DAYS.

*B.*
I KNOW THE SECRETS OF THE HIEROGLYPHS AND HOW TO MIX PIGMENTS. BECAUSE I AM AN EXCELLENT CRAFTSMAN, I KNOW HOW TO CREATE THE POSTURE OF A MAN'S STATUE AND FORM THE GRACE OF A WOMAN'S STATUE, HOW TO SHOW BIRDS IN FLIGHT OR THE SPEED OF THE RUNNER.

*C.*
HIS MAJESTY COMMANDED MY WEAPONS TRAINING, TOGETHER WITH SIX MEN OF HIS PALACE.... IN BATTLE I GUARDED THE REAR OF THE ARMY AND WHEN WE FOUGHT AGAINST THE ASIATICS, I ATTACKED AND NEVER CEASED FROM THE FIGHT. BLESS MY EYES, I NEVER RAN AWAY. HIS MAJESTY REWARDED ME HIMSELF AND GAVE ME A THROW STICK, A DAGGER, AND A SHEATH ALL WORKED IN GOLD.

ANSWERS: A. Doctor, B. Draughtsman, C. Soldier

# ANCIENT EGYPTIAN WORKERS: FACT AND MYTH

MYTH: The Egyptians used thousands of slaves to build their monuments.
FACT: Slavery was rare in Ancient Egypt. However, there was a system by which ordinary people owed a certain portion of their working life to the pharaoh, a bit like military service.

MYTH: Women didn't work outside the home.
FACT: Although many women did devote themselves to running their household and the task of bearing children, some women occupied the most prestigious and responsible positions in Egypt, including that of pharaoh.

MYTH: Workers were paid in gold.
FACT: There was no equivalent of our currency in Ancient Egypt. A barter system was used in which goods like grain, oil, cattle, or copper were valued against each other. For example, one pig might be worth five copper rings.

MYTH: The workers were driven very hard and had no holidays.
FACT: Records show people at Deir El Medina had two days off after eight days of work and that a working day was eight hours long with a lunch break. Records also show that they sometimes went on strike.

Lesson 15

# Fun and Games in Ancient Egypt

Archaeological evidence shows that the Ancient Egyptians knew how to live the good life. Not only did they love feasting, music, and dancing, but they also enjoyed a whole range of games and sport. Everyone, from the royal family to the poorest peasant, would have played the popular board games Dogs and Jackals (a bit like Snakes and Ladders) and Senet, although not everyone would own an inlaid ebony and ivory playing board like Tutankhamen's!

*Senet was a game for two players, a bit like our game of backgammon. The aim was to move pieces round the board to the last five squares and then remove them.*

Children would have played many different games — some of which are still familiar, like marbles or catch. In one game, players tried to jump over the linked arms of their opponents. In another, children played catch sitting on the back of a teammate.

*Young children might have played with a doll made of rags and papyrus, or a toy animal made of wood with moving parts, like this cat.*

*It is likely that children loved listening to stories. Some people believe this papyrus from Thebes could be the first ever children's book.*

ACTIVITY: Find your way through the marshes to hunt ducks. You mustn't go down a channel that ends in a crocodile or hippo, and watch out for your vizier, who is hiding to make sure you have an "accident" so he can replace you as pharaoh. Answer on page 43.

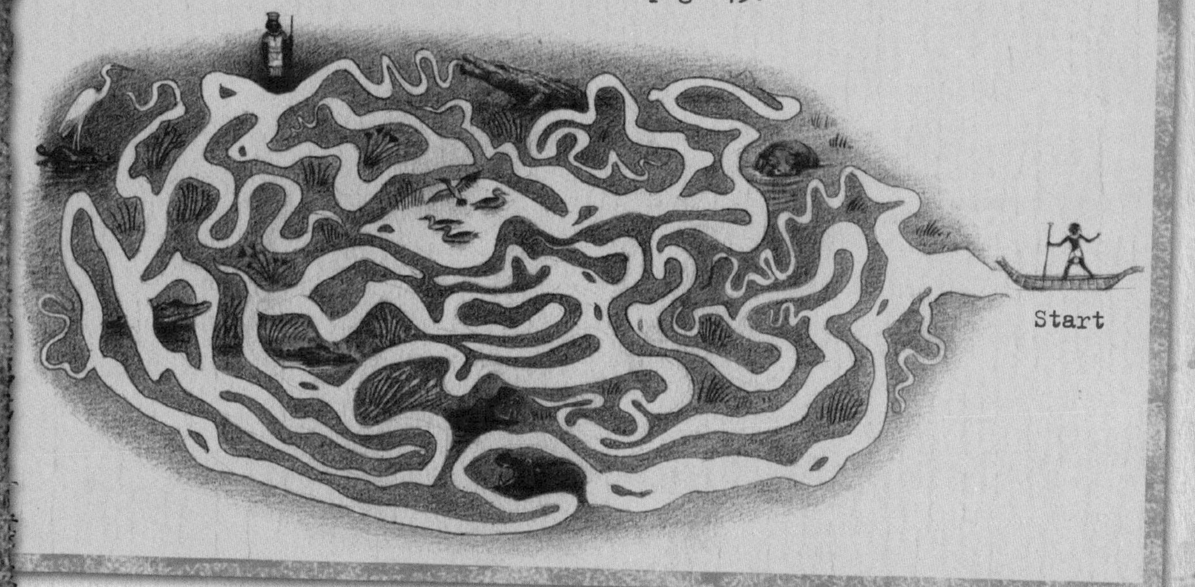

## Lesson 16
# Travel and Trade in Ancient Egypt

The Ancient Egyptians didn't enjoy travel, partly because they believed that Egypt was the best land in the whole world and partly because if they died abroad, they would not be able to receive a proper Egyptian burial. However, although Egypt was a wealthy country, it lacked some necessities, and expeditions were organised to exchange Egypt's gold, grain, and other goods for wood, precious stones, spices, incense, silver, and tin.

THE EXPEDITION TO PUNT

The Pharaoh Hatshepsut ordered an expedition to an African land known as Punt, which might have been on the Red Sea coast. It was rich in the incense, perfumes, and resins needed for temple ritual and mummification.

*Hatshepsut was so proud of her expedition that she commissioned pictures of it to be added to the walls of her mortuary temple at Deir El Bahri. The sketches you see here, however, are copies of sketches made around one hundred years ago, for now the colouring is almost too faded to see.*

ACTIVITY: Imagine you are travelling to Punt to buy 6 animal skins for your priests, 20 incense trees, and 35 precious gems. Work out how many Egyptian goods — such as honey, grain, gold, and cloth — you might need to take with you to Punt.

| Goods from Egypt | | Goods from Punt |
|---|---|---|
| 1 gold ring =<br>1/2 sack grain =<br>30 jars honey =<br>10 linen shirts | are worth the same as | 4 incense trees =<br>3 leopard skins =<br>7 precious stones |

SUGGESTED ANSWER: You could take 2 gold rings to exchange for the 6 leopard skins, 2 1/2 sacks of grain to exchange for the incense trees, and 50 linen shirts to exchange for the 35 precious stones.

## *Lesson 17*

# *Palace Life*

Today we know more about Ancient Egyptian tombs than we know about their palaces because the palaces were largely made of mud brick and were not built to last for eternity. Excavations show that the king's vast palaces provided a luxurious home for the king and his family. They were also the centre of government and the base for the king's court, his vizier, and all the nobles who surrounded the king in the hope of gaining royal favour.

*The royal family, Pharaoh Akhenaten, Queen Nefertiti, and their daughters, distribute "gold of honour" to royal favourites from the Window of Appearances in their palace at Akhetaten.*

RUNNING THE PALACE

Maintaining the highest standards of comfort and luxury was a full-time job for the workers in the palace kitchens, storerooms, workshops, and offices. The pharaoh must have had hundreds or even thousands of servants, each with his or her own particular duties to ensure the smooth running of the enormous royal household!

ACTIVITY: Look at this overhead view of the royal palace of King Akhenaten. Can you label the following rooms on the plan: royal bedroom, treasure chamber, shrine, and throne room?

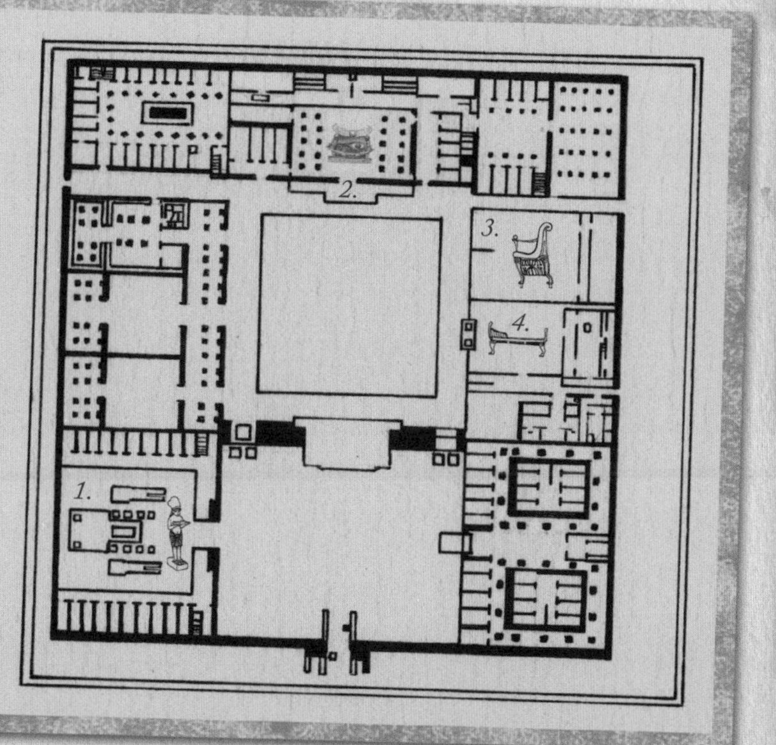


ANSWERS: 1. Shrine
2. Treasure chamber
3. Throne room
4. Royal bedroom

PALACE RICHES

The pharaoh was also the wealthiest person in Ancient Egypt, and his royal treasury would have been overflowing with riches — produce from his land as well as taxes and tribute sent from foreign rulers. Sometimes the gifts from overseas included exotic animals for the king's personal botanical gardens and zoo!

## Lesson 18

# Ancient Egyptian Warfare

Although the Ancient Egyptians of the Old and Middle Kingdoms did go to war, it wasn't until the New Kingdom that Egypt became an advanced military power. By this time, the army had more sophisticated weapons, including the wheeled chariot and a composite bow. The army itself was made up of a mixture of conscripts, professional Egyptian soldiers, and foreign mercenaries, all under the command of a general who in turn answered to the pharaoh himself.

*Rameses II in his war chariot*

THE MAKEUP OF THE ARMY

The army of Rameses II was divided into four divisions of 5,000 men. These were divided in turn into 20 companies of 250 men. Finally there were five smaller groups of 50 soldiers, each of whom answered to their captain, the "greatest of fifty."

*This scene, from Rameses II's temple at Abu Simbel, shows the king single-handedly charging the enemy at the Battle of Kadesh. This battle led to a peace treaty between the Hittites and the Ancient Egyptians.*

ACTIVITY: Identify these common Egyptian weapons of the New and Middle Kingdoms. Choose from: axe, spear, dagger, throw stick, Khepesh sword, bow and arrow.

1.

2.

3.

4.

5.

6.

ANSWERS: 1. Khepesh sword 2. Dagger 3. Throw stick, 4. Axe 5. Bow and arrow 6. Spear.

## Lesson 19

# Reading Hieroglyphs

The meaning of hieroglyphs, the Ancient Egyptian sacred writings, was unknown until the signs were deciphered in the nineteenth century, thanks to the discovery of an essential key by French soldiers: a block of carved granite that came to be called the Rosetta Stone. This stone had an ancient decree written on it in three scripts: Ancient Greek; demotic, the common script of Egypt; and hieroglyphic, the Egyptian sacred script used by priests and scribes.

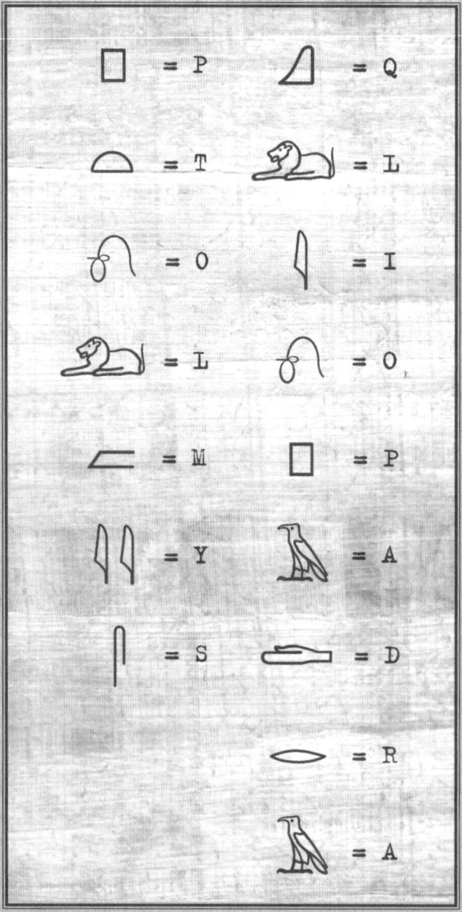

| | |
|---|---|
| = P | = Q |
| = T | = L |
| = O | = I |
| = L | = O |
| = M | = P |
| = Y | = A |
| = S | = D |
| | = R |
| | = A |

CHAMPOLLION

The man who finally deciphered the Rosetta Stone was Jean François Champollion. He realised that most hieroglyphs did not stand for whole words but for sounds, which he transliterated into the letters of our alphabet that represented roughly similar sounds. He also discovered that special names — such as the names of pharaohs — were recorded in ovals called cartouches. By comparing the three texts on the Rosetta Stone, and by comparing two names on the stone to the same names on an obelisk from Philae, he was first able to identify two royal names — Ptolemy and Cleopatra.

*The picture above shows the name Rameses-meryamun, one of the names of Rameses II, the king who built Abu Simbel. As was usual, the name of the god Amun is written first, although it is pronounced last.*

ACTIVITY: Translate these names of nineteenth-dynasty pharaohs.

Note: You will find all the signs you need to help you on the next page.

= PR

= AA

*Right: The king of Egypt came to be called pharaoh by the Greeks, from the title Per Aa meaning "Great House."*

## Lesson 20
# Writing Hieroglyphs

Ancient Egyptian hieroglyphs are made up of picture symbols. Most symbols stand for sounds and can be combined to make up a word. For example, the symbol (r) and the symbol (n) could be combined to make the word (rn), meaning "name." We have no idea how the Ancient Egyptians pronounced this word, so for convenience we add an "e" between the letters to make it easier to say as "ren."

Here are the basic SINGLE-LETTER signs:

| | | |
|---|---|---|
| a | i | q |
| a | j | r |
| b | kh | sh |
| d | kh | or s |
| f | k | tj |
| g | m | t |
| h | n | w/u |
| h | p | y |

As well as these single-letter hieroglyphs, we have some hieroglyphs that represent more than one letter, for example the symbols (pr), (nfr), and (ankh). Again, we add an "e" to the first two so we can pronounce them as "per" and "nefer."

Here are some signs made up of TWO or THREE sylables:

| | | |
|---|---|---|
| aa | nb | djd |
| wr | ib | sw |
| jw | mr | ntjr |
| thut | ms | mn |
| khnm | hat | shpsy |
| akh | hka | iun |
| shma | ankh | mr |

Most Egyptian hieroglyphs represent sounds or sound combinations, which are put together to make words, just like the letters in our own alphabet. However, there is another kind of symbol used by the Ancient Egyptians, called a determinative. These symbols represent a thing or an idea and were usually put at the end of a word to show what kind of word it was. For example, if you see the symbol ⊗ in a word, it means that the word is the name of a town or a place, while stands for motion. Here are the names of two Ancient Egyptian towns: Djedu (Busiris) and Abdju (Abydos).

Here are some DETERMINATIVE signs:

| | | | |
|---|---|---|---|
| man | woman | motion | weak, small |
| god | sun, Ra | plural | abstract idea |

ANSWERS TO PHARAOH HIEROGLYPHS

1. Thutmosis (thut-ms-s)
2. Khenmetamun-hatshepsut(khnm-t-i-mn-n hat-shpsy)
3. Akhenaten (akh-kh-n-i-t-n + "sun" symbol)
4. Tutankhamen-hekaiunushema (t-u-t-ankh-i-mn-n hka-iun-shma)
5. Rameses-meryamun (ra-ms-s-sw mr-i-mn-n)

Remember Ptah, Aten, and Amun are usually written first!

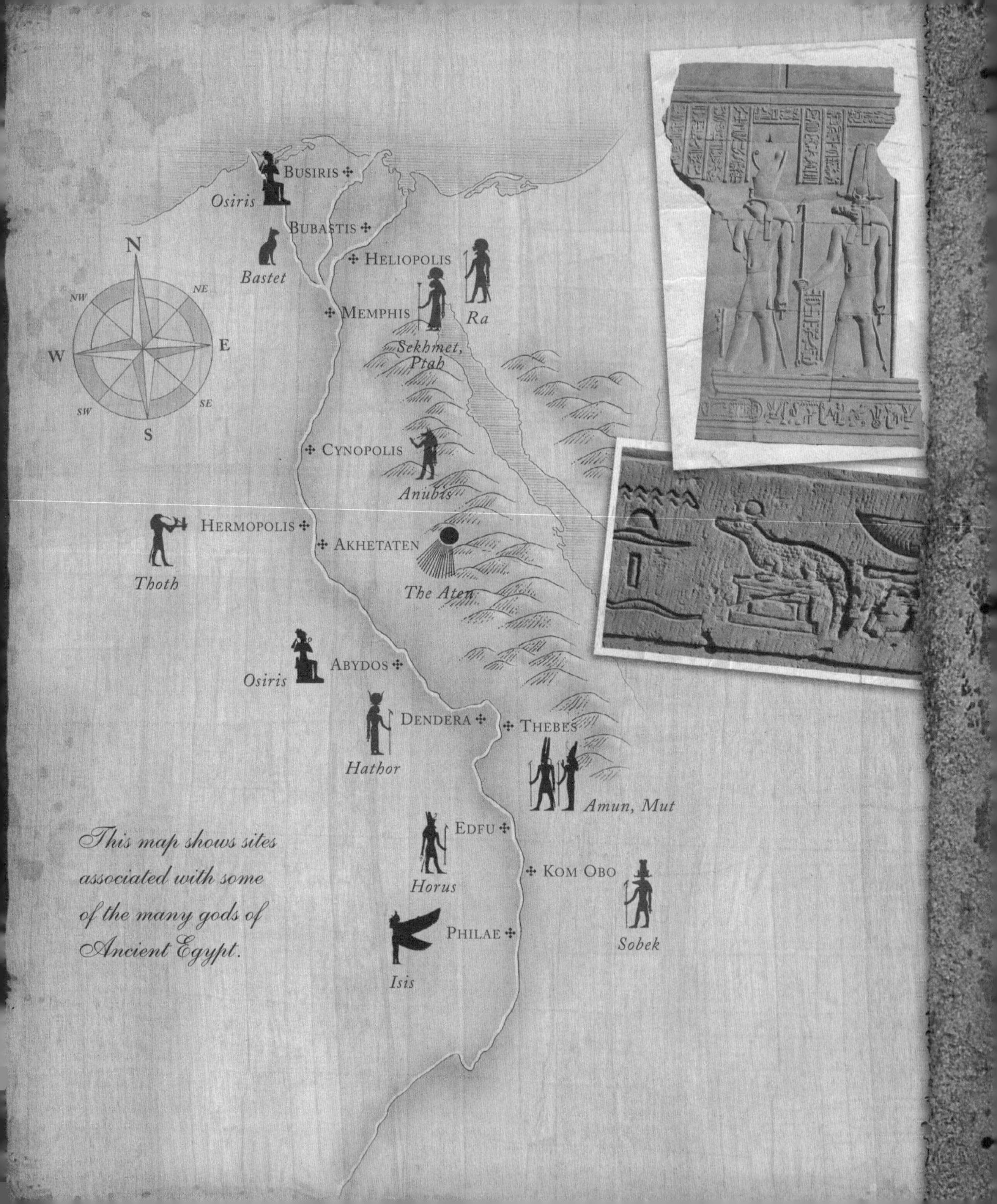


*This map shows sites associated with some of the many gods of Ancient Egypt.*

*Part III*

# *Gods and Religion in Ancient Egypt*

The Ancient Egyptians believed in many gods and many different kinds of gods. There were national gods, such as Amun, Mut, Ptah, and Ra, and there were also local gods linked to one's own town or city. There were gods associated with certain beasts, such as Sobek, the crocodile god. And there were also gods associated with certain jobs, such as Anubis, god of embalmers, and gods associated with certain aspects of life and death, such as Osiris, the lord of the underworld. Having so many gods meant that Ancient Egypt was a land full of temples, and one where there were a great many festivals and celebrations!

*You rise in beauty on the horizon of heaven,*<br>
*O living Aten, the source of life!*<br>
*When you have risen on the eastern horizon,*<br>
*You have filled every land with your beauty.*<br>
*You are beautiful, great, radiant,*<br>
*High over every land.*<br>
*"The Hymn to the Aten," c. 1330 BC*

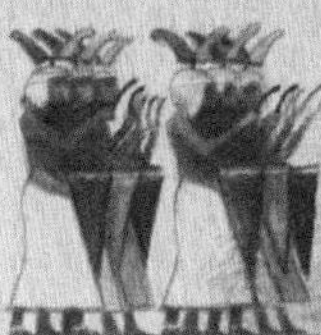

## Lesson 21

# The Many Gods of Ancient Egypt

Although Ancient Egyptians worshipped many different gods, an ordinary Egyptian wouldn't have prayed to all these gods at once. Instead, there might have been a local god or "family" of gods who were the main focus of worship. Other gods would have been asked for help at specific times. For example, the goddess Taweret was seen as the protector of women during childbirth, and Bes was the protector of the home, while Osiris, left, was lord of the afterlife.

*The Ancient Egyptians built many temples, such as this one at Philae—seen before it was engulfed by the waters held back by the 1902 Aswan Dam.*

ACTIVITY: Ancient Egyptian gods often came in "triads" of three gods — a father, a mother, and a child. Can you match each god to the correct description for the triad below?

Amun was worshipped at Thebes as king of the gods.
Mut, a mother goddess, was sometimes shown as a vulture.
Khonsu, the moon god, had a child's sidelock of hair.

ANSWERS: 1. Khonsu 2. Amun 3. Mut

ISIS AND OSIRIS

Ancient Egyptians believed that Egypt was once ruled by Osiris and his wife and sister, Isis, until the couple's jealous brother Seth killed Osiris, hiding parts of his body in different places.

*Transforming herself into a kite, Isis collected the parts of her dead husband's body and breathed life back into them. She is called the mistress of magic.*

*Osiris, the murdered king, became lord of the underworld after his death. He is often shown with green skin, which represents rebirth and regeneration.*

*Hawk-headed Horus was the son of Isis and Osiris. He began a long battle with Seth, finally defeating him to become king of Egypt. Later kings identified themselves as Horus.*

*Seth was the god of the desert and of storms. As the murderer of Osiris, he was feared for his brutal ferocity and yet admired for his strength and cunning.*

# *Lesson 22*
# *An Ancient Egyptian Myth*

This tale, THE STORY OF RA, tells of the creation of the earth, and of how the god Ra grew angry with humankind and tried to destroy them using his daughter, the terrible goddess Sekhmet.

In the beginning there was the all-powerful god, Ra. He made the other gods: Shu — the winds that blew, Tefnut — the rain that fell, Geb — the earth, and Nut — the sky goddess. And Ra also made the god Hapi — the River Nile that flowed and made Egypt fertile. Then Ra made all things on earth and he also made humans. Ra ruled as pharaoh for thousands of years, and it was such a time of goodness and plenty that people spoke of it fondly forever after.

But it came to pass that Ra grew old, and people no longer feared or obeyed him. So Ra became angry and summoned all the other gods to him. They advised him, "Send destruction upon humankind and turn your Eye against them."

So Ra sent his Eye against them, in the form of his daughter Sekhmet, the fiercest and most terrible of all the goddesses. Like a lion rushing upon its prey, she fell upon the people of Upper and Lower Egypt and slew all those who had disobeyed her father, Ra. She killed everyone she saw and rejoiced in the slaughter, delighting in the taste of blood.

The Nile itself ran red with blood, and eventually Ra felt sorry for the people, but even he couldn't stop Sekhmet's bloodthirsty rampage, so carried away was she with her terrible cruelty.

Ra realised he would have to trick Sekhmet into stopping, so he ordered messengers to take red ochre from the isle of Elephantine and then bring it to him in the town of Heliopolis, where the women had been brewing beer all day long at Ra's command. The red ochre was mixed with seven thousand jars of beer and then poured out over the land where Sekhmet was planning her next slaughter.

When the sun rose the next day, Sekhmet saw the ground all flooded with the red beer, and, thinking it was the blood of those she had killed, she laughed with joy and drank deeply of it. She drank so much that the strength of the beer made her powerless. She could no longer slay, but instead she slept the day away and then staggered back to her father.

Ra said, "You come in peace, sweet one," and from that moment onwards she became the goddess Hathor, as sweet and strong as love itself. Each new year afterwards, the priestesses of Hathor drank the beer of Heliopolis coloured with red ochre from Elephantine to celebrate her festival.

Ra continued to rule, but he was growing old and losing his wisdom. None of the other gods could take his wisdom as they didn't know his secret name of power. But then Geb and Nut had children, and the younger gods and goddesses were born: Osiris, Isis, Seth, and Nephthys. Isis was the wisest of these four, and she managed to trick Ra into telling her his secret name of power.

From that time on, Ra was pharaoh no longer but took his place in the heavens, travelling across the sky each day and crossing the underworld each night in the Boat of Ra, taking with him the souls of the dead.

## Lesson 23

# Everyday Gods of Ancient Egypt

Egyptologists need to be able to recognise Ancient Egyptian gods and goddesses, even in the darkest tomb. To assist with this, they should memorise my simple chart (right) before attempting to match the gods below with their names and descriptions.

SEKHMET: *The lion-headed goddess of vengeance, who leads the pharaoh into battle*

HATHOR: *The cow-horned goddess of love, fertility, music, and dance*

SOBEK: *The powerful, crocodile-headed god of the Nile*

THOTH: *The ibis-headed god of wisdom; the patron of scribes*

ANUBIS: *The jackal-headed god; the patron of embalmers*

BES: *The bearded dwarf who guards the home against evil*

BASTET: *The cat goddess who is protector of the home and of domestic cats*

Emily Sands says:
"Know Your Ancient Egyptian Gods."
The success of an excavation or even finding the right site may depend on your familiarity with this chart showing many of the most popular Ancient Egyptian gods.
RA
Sun God
OSIRIS
God of the Underworld
ISIS
Wife of Osiris
HORUS
Son of Osiris
SETH
Evil Brother of Osiris
THOTH
God of Scribes and Wisdom
HATHOR
Goddess of Music and Love
SOBEK
God of Crocodiles
SEKHMET
Goddess of Vengeance
ANUBIS
God of Embalmers
BASTET
Goddess of Cats and the Home
BES
God of the Household

## Lesson 24

# An Ancient Egyptian Temple

Ancient Egyptian temples were called the "mansions of the gods." There, statues of the gods were carefully tended by priests and servants. The closest ordinary people might come was the outer temple courtyard, and only during special festivals. The temple grew progressively more sacred towards its centre. Only priests of the highest level and the king himself were allowed to approach the sanctuary, where the god's sacred shrine, or "naos," was found.

TEMPLE WORSHIP

Three times each day, the high priest attended the god, making offerings of food, drink, perfume, and flowers. He would enter the sanctuary and take the god's statue from its shrine. There, he would remove the statue's clothes and clean it, applying fresh eye paint and dressing it in new clothing. Finally, food and drink would be presented for the god's symbolic meal. However, fish was considered an unacceptable offering.

*Above: The priests dress the statue of Horus in the temple at Edfu.*

The impressive exterior of the Temple of Horus at Edfu: you can see its main front pylons decorated with vast reliefs showing Ptolemy XII (who completed its construction) in the presence of the god Horus and his consort, Hathor.

*When we visited the amazingly well-preserved Temple of Horus, it was not difficult to imagine how imposing it must have been in its day.*

*1. Pylon entrance*
*2. Courtyard*
*3. Hypostyle hall*
*4. Antechamber*
*5. Naos or shrine*

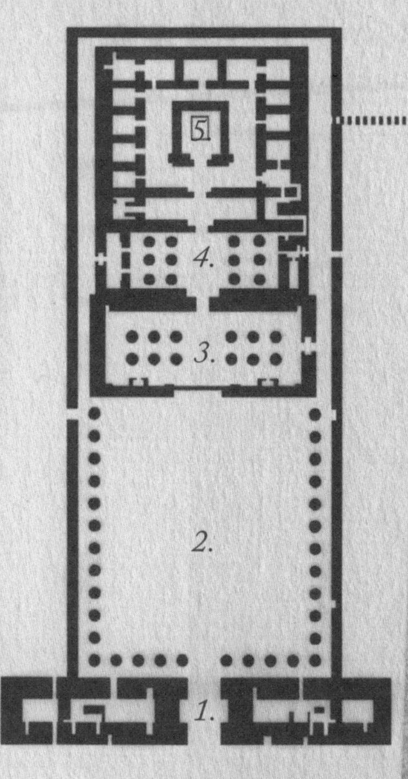


*The Temple of Horus at Edfu*

ACTIVITY: Guess which four of these things might have been among the offerings placed before Horus in the temple at Edfu.

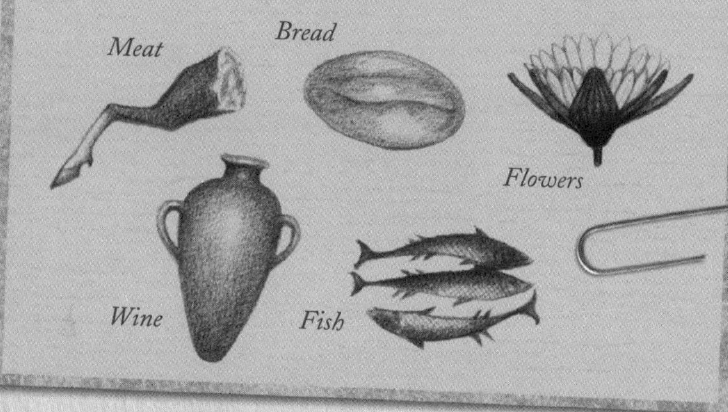


ANSWER: Fish was not an acceptable offering.

## Lesson 25

# Religious Festivals in Ancient Egypt

As well as the secret temple rituals, another important part of Ancient Egyptian religious life was the celebration of annual festivals — more than fifty a year. The Ancient Egyptians used a 365-day calendar like ours. However, it was divided into 360 regular days plus five sacred days devoted to Osiris, Isis, Horus, Seth, and Nephthys.

THE FESTIVAL OF THE BEAUTIFUL MEETING
This festival celebrated the marriage of the god Horus to Hathor. The statue of Horus from the temple at Edfu was taken to meet Hathor's statue — which was brought by river from Dendera, 100 miles away. The feast included free food and drink for all pilgrims. I'm sure it was a very popular celebration!

THE OPET FESTIVAL

The Opet Festival honoured the gods of Karnak in a lively celebration that renewed the pharaoh's powers. The gods' images were carried by boat from Karnak to the temple at Luxor. At Luxor temple, the king withdrew with the statues for a secret rite. The Opet Festival gave ordinary Egyptians the chance to consult an oracle: When a statue passed, people could ask a question. It would dip for "yes" or back away for "no."

THE SED FESTIVAL

Every thirty years, a pharaoh had to perform the Sed Festival (shown above) to show he was still powerful enough to rule Egypt. How much can you find out about this festival?

*Lesson 26*

# *Life After Death*

By the time of the New Kingdom, Ancient Egyptians had come to believe in the existence of an afterlife, which curiously enough was very much like Egypt. This land, where the souls of the dead enjoyed everlasting life with Osiris, its ruler, was called the Field of Reeds. It was a place of happiness and plenty, where crops grew abundantly, work was easy, and life was pleasant.

## TOMB BURIALS

When a mummy had been taken to its tomb, the priests carried out a ceremony called the Opening of the Mouth. This enabled the dead person's "ba," or soul, to travel out of the body. In another part of the ceremony, objects were offered that the deceased would need in the next life.

*These illustrations show the Opening of the Mouth ceremony being performed on a mummy (above) and Horus leading a dead man named Ani into the presence of Osiris, the god of the afterlife (left).*

## THE JUDGMENT OF THE DEAD

It was believed that the dead would be judged to see if they were "true of voice." Each dead person's heart was weighed against the feather of Maat, or truth. Anubis placed it on the scales, while ibis-headed Thoth, the god of wisdom, recorded the verdict.

ACTIVITY: At the judgment of the soul, Ancient Egyptians believed they had to make what is called a "negative confession." This meant that they had to list a series of bad things they had NOT done while they were alive. One of the following statements is not a negative confession. Be careful: if you are wrong, Thoth may release Ammat the devourer!

1. "I have not killed a man."
2. "I have borrowed the pharaoh's favourite perfume."
3. "I have not let any man go hungry."
4. "I have not purloined the cakes of the gods."
5. "I have not taken milk from the mouths of babies."
6. "I have not driven away beasts from their pastures."

ANSWER: 2 is not a negative confession

*Lesson 27*

# *Ancient Egyptian Mummies*

In predynastic times, Egyptians buried their dead in the dry sand, which preserved them, often for thousands of years. But sometimes, desert animals would dig up the bodies, so they began to place the bodies in coffins. Unfortunately, bodies in coffins rot easily. Thus was born the process of protecting bodies by first embalming them and then mummifying them.

*To prepare the body for embalming, various organs were removed, including the brain, which was extracted through the nose with a tool called a brain hook.*

*At first, only pharaohs were mummified. This picture shows the mummy of Rameses II. Later, the technique became available to ordinary people as well.*

## CANOPIC JARS

After the organs were removed from the body they were placed in canopic jars protected by four gods: jackal-headed Duamutef (stomach), human-headed Imsety (liver), baboon-headed Hapi (lungs), and falcon-headed Qebehsenuef (intestines).

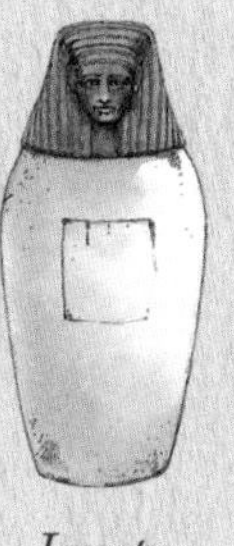

*Imsety*

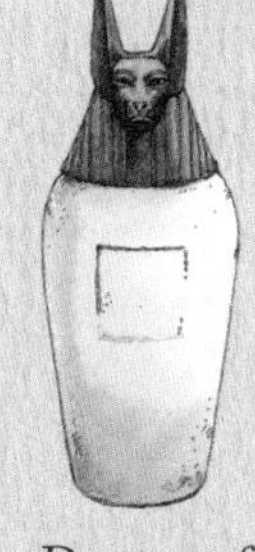

*Duamutef*

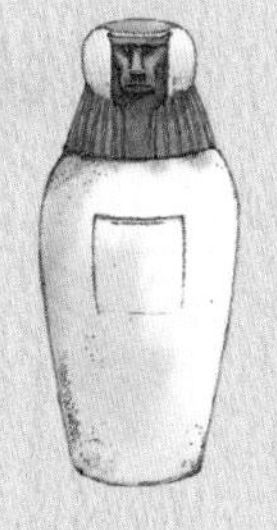

*Hapi*

*Qebehsenuef*

## THE PROCESS OF MUMMIFICATION

The process usually followed these steps for pharaohs and rich people: First, the body was washed and the organs were removed. These were preserved in canopic jars, except for the brain, which was thrown away. Second, the corpse was covered in a salt called natron and left to dry for 40 days. Third, the body was wrapped in linen. Finally, the body was wrapped in a sheet.

ACTIVITY: Place these pictures in the correct order.

*A*

*B*

*C*

*D*

ANSWER: D, B, C, A

## Lesson 28

# The Burial of a King

A royal burial was a vast undertaking and its organisation — including building the tomb and creating the precious objects to be buried alongside the mummy — might have taken decades. Kings would have started preparations for their funerals when they were still young. The final arrangements were made while the body was undergoing its 70-day mummification process. When the mummy was ready for burial, an elaborate funeral procession carried it to its resting place.

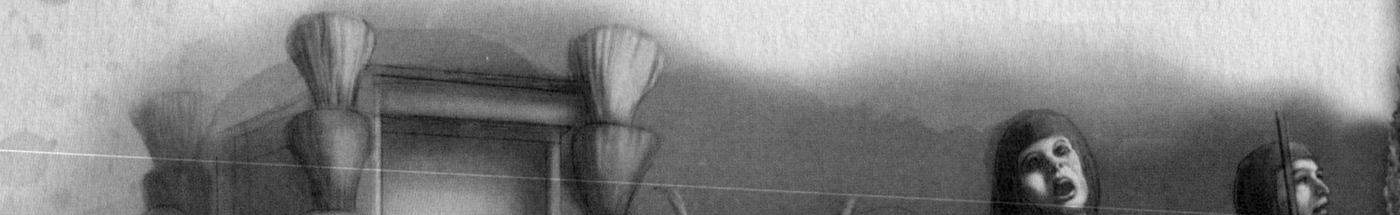

The king's mummy inside its golden coffin was laid on a sledge and pulled along by oxen. Professional mourners joined the procession, weeping, wailing, and putting dirt on their heads. Priests were needed to carry out the appropriate rituals, burning incense and making offerings. Items the dead person needed for the afterlife were taken to be buried with them.

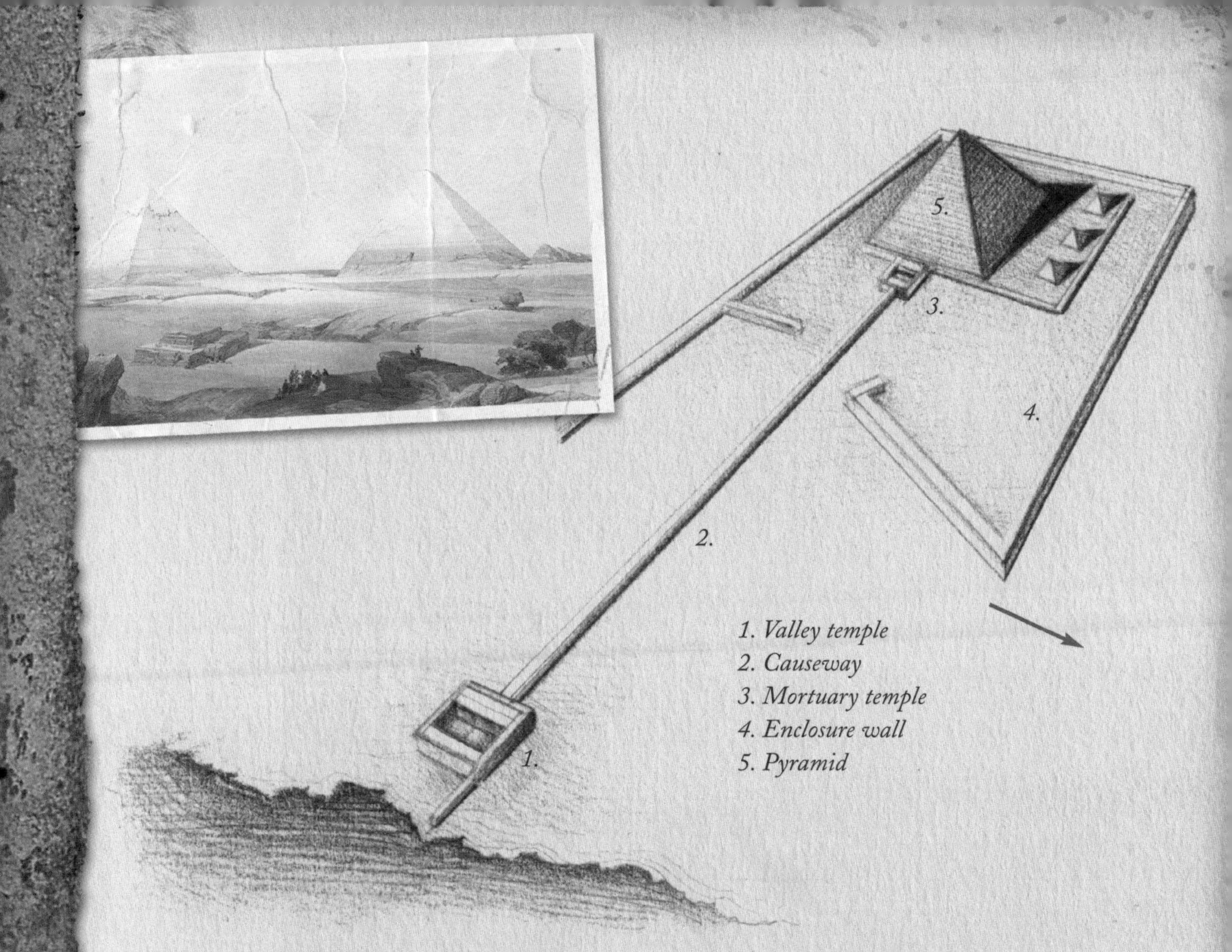


*King Menkaura's body was brought by boat to his valley temple on the banks of a canal cut from the Nile. Next, it was taken in procession along the covered causeway linking the valley temple to the main pyramid complex. Inside the walls of the main complex was a mortuary temple where the mummy was placed for the funeral ceremonies and where the cult of the dead king would make offerings. Finally, the mummy was laid to rest in its burial chamber in the main pyramid.*

ACTIVITY: From the description, trace the course the king's funeral procession would have taken from his valley temple to his burial chamber in the pyramid on the plan above.

## Lesson 29

# Animal Mummies and the Serapeum

Humans were not the only creatures to be mummified in Ancient Egypt. The Serapeum at Saqqara is just one of many catacombs containing the mummified remains of animals and birds. Discovered in 1851 by the famous French archaeologist Auguste Mariette, its crypts house enormous coffins hewn from single granite blocks, specially shaped to hold the mummies of the sacred Apis bulls.

*An Apis bull was worshipped as the living incarnation of the god Ptah.*

### THE SERAPEUM

The Serapeum was extended by Prince Khaemwese, one of the many sons of Rameses II. As a high priest of Ptah, Khaemwese was in charge of caring for the Apis bulls. Some people believe a mummy found in the Serapeum is that of Khaemwese, who died before he could inherit his father's throne.

*Mummified animals were sometimes placed in bronze coffins like the one on the left.*

Animals were associated with certain gods, and so people might purchase a mummified animal to take to a temple as an offering to a particular god. When some of these mummies were recently unwrapped, a few were found to be fakes. There were obviously some dishonest mummy dealers in Ancient Egypt!

ACTIVITY: Can you guess which animals have been mummified inside these bandages? They are a cat, an ibis, a baboon, a snake, and an Apis bull.

ANSWERS: 1. Baboon 2. Cat 3. Apis bull 4. Ibis 5. Snake

## Lesson 30

# The Amarna Heresy

The Amarna period, during the rule of the "heretic pharaoh," Akhenaten, continues to puzzle and divide scholars. During this time, Amenhotep IV banned the worship of Ancient Egypt's many traditional gods in favour of the worship of just one god — the Aten. He changed his name to Akhenaten and set up a brand-new capital city halfway between Memphis and Thebes at Tel el Amarna called Akhetaten, or the "horizon of the Aten."

KING AKHENATEN

In representations of him from the Amarna period, Akhenaten has an unusual appearance — his head is very elongated, for example. This has led some scholars to wonder if he suffered from some kind of physical deformity. Others believe that there was nothing wrong with Akhenaten's physique, but rather that this art style — like so much else in the reign of this extraordinary king — was distinctive as a drastic break from tradition.

*This sketch in the Amarna style shows a relief of Akhenaten that was found on one of the walls of the capital city that he built, Akhetaten. It shows the king, his wife, Nefertiti, and their daughters worshipping the Aten, which is represented on the relief as the rays of the sun.*

WHAT BECAME OF AKHENATEN

When Akhenaten died, it didn't take long for the country to return to the old religion and former capital city. Later generations reacted violently against this heretic king, and his name and monuments were defaced to obliterate all trace of him. The fact that we remember the boy-king who was probably Akhenaten's son as Tutankhamen, "Living Image of Amun," rather than by his original name of Tutankhaten, "Living Image of the Aten," shows how immediate and complete the reversal of the Akhenaten's Amarna revolution was.

ACTIVITY: Names were very important in ancient Egypt. Amenhotep IV ("Amun Is at Peace") changed his name to Akhenaten ("Servant of the Aten"). Using your knowledge of Egyptian gods, can you work out which of these names belong to the Amarna period?

1. Meritaten ("The Aten's Beloved")
2. Ptahhotep ("Ptah Is at Peace")
3. Sithathor ("Daughter of Hathor")
4. Ankhesenpaaten ("May She Live for the Aten")

ANSWER: 1 and 4

## Appendix 1

# A Chronology of Egyptian History

NOTE: Dates in the history of Ancient Egypt are usually estimates, especially for the earliest periods.

PREDYNASTIC PERIOD, 5000–3200 BC

ARCHAIC PERIOD, 3200–2650 BC

2950 BC Earliest written texts at Abydos

2900 BC Reign of NARMER (Menes?), first king of United Egypt. The country's capital is established at Memphis.

OLD KINGDOM, 2650–2150 BC

2630 BC Step Pyramid of ZOSER, the first monumental stone building in the world, built by Imhotep

2550 BC Great Pyramid of KHUFU, followed by the pyramids of KHAEFRA and MENKAURA at Giza

2150 BC The death of PEPI II, after lengthy 94-year reign, marks the end of the Old Kingdom.

FIRST INTERMEDIATE PERIOD, 2150–2040 BC

2150 BC Central power breaks down, leading to political chaos in Egypt. The kingdom is no longer united under one king.

MIDDLE KINGDOM, 2040–1750 BC

2040 BC The Theban MENTUHOTEP II becomes king of a reunited Egypt. Thebes becomes the new capital.

1750 BC The Middle Kingdom comes to a gradual end, as 13th-dynasty kings lose control of the country.

SECOND INTERMEDIATE PERIOD, 1750–1550 BC

1650 BC Foreign Hyksos rulers, who built a kingdom in the north around Avaris, capture Memphis.

1540 BC KAMOSE, king of Thebes, leads his army in a raid on the city of Avaris.

NEW KINGDOM, 1550–1070 BC

1550 BC King AHMOSE reunites Egypt at the start of the New Kingdom.

1500 BC THUTMOSIS I initiates the Valley of the Kings and founds the village at Deir El Medina.

1480 BC Queen HATSHEPSUT ascends the throne.

1450 BC Under THUTMOSIS III Egyptian rule extends as far as the Euphrates River in the west.

1350 BC AMENHOTEP IV renames himself AKHENATEN, bans the worship of Egypt's old gods in favour of the Aten, and builds a new capital at Akhetaten.

1330 BC The cults of the old gods are restored under TUTANKHAMEN. Thebes becomes the capital of Egypt once again.

1275 BC RAMESES II fights the Hittites at the Battle of Kadesh. He builds many monuments to himself, including the temple at Abu Simbel.

1180 BC RAMESES III repels the invasion of the Sea Peoples. He is the last great pharaoh of Egypt.

LATE NEW KINGDOM, 1070–712 BC

1070 BC The lessening power of the king leads to a loss of central control and Assyrian domination.

LATE PERIOD, 712–332

664 BC PSAMTEK I reunites Egypt, but it eventually falls to Persian, then Graeco-Roman kings.

GRAECO-ROMAN PERIOD, 332 BC–AD 395

332 BC ALEXANDER invades Egypt. Subsequently Egypt is ruled by the Ptolemys, the last of whom was CLEOPATRA VII.

*Appendix 2*

# *A Brief History of Egyptology*

The first historians and archaeologists to be fascinated by Ancient Egypt were the Ancient Egyptians themselves. Travellers and tourists from the Old Kingdom onwards left traces of their presence at sites of historical interest, and some monuments were positively covered with Ancient Greek and Roman graffiti. European interest in Egypt began to develop after Napoleon's armies opened up the country in the early nineteenth century, and the scholars or "savants" who travelled with Napoleon began recording the many wonderful things that they found.

Giovanni Battista Belzoni
1778–1823

*Belzoni shipped many fine pieces of statue back to England, but his methods often resulted in damage.*

Auguste Mariette
1821–1881

*Auguste Mariette excavated many sites and founded the Antiquities Service and Egyptian Museum.*

Amelia B. Edwards
1831–1892

*Amelia B. Edwards wrote an account of her journey to Egypt and founded the Egypt Exploration Fund.*

William Matthew Flinders Petrie
1853–

*Flinders Petrie developed many new archaeological methods, such as using pottery in sequence dating.*

Howard Carter
1874–

*Howard Carter made a name for himself by finding and excavating the tomb of Tutankhamen.*

## A CHRONOLOGY OF EARLY EGYPTOLOGY

1400 BC The prince who was to become Thutmosis IV clears away the sand that has built up around the Sphinx.

1280 BC Prince Khaemwese, son of Rameses II, has inscriptions carved on some of the ancient monuments at Saqqara to record that he restored them in his father's name.

450 BC Greek historian Herodotus writes a contemporary account of Ancient Egypt in "The Histories."

300 BC The Egyptian priest Manetho writes a "History of Egypt," dividing his lists of the kings into 30 dynasties.

1150 AD An Iraqi doctor, Abd el-Latif, writes of his journey around the ancient sites of Egypt.

1639 AD English mathematician John Greaves makes the first scientific survey of the Giza Plateau.

1745 AD The Reverend Richard Pococke publishes a two-volume account of his voyage to Egypt.

1790 AD James Bruce publishes his "Travels to Discover the Source of the Nile."

1798 AD Napoleon's ships arrive with a corps of 167 scholars, who aim to record every detail of the country in "Description de L'Egypte."

1822 AD Frenchman Jean François Champollion writes his "Lettre à M. Dacier," which outlines the method for translating hieroglyphs.

The "Bennu Bird"
5th January 1927

My Dearest Niece and Nephew,

Now that you have read my book, you should know something about Egyptology and about the history of Ancient Egypt. One of the reasons it is so exciting is that Egyptologists from museums and universities all over the world are making new discoveries all the time. Without their work, many priceless antiquities and finds that help us understand the lives of people who lived many thousands of years in the past might be lost.

For example, in order to control the flooding of the Nile, the Egyptian authorities have had to build a dam across the river near the first cataract at Aswan. As the water has risen behind this dam, it has began to cover many important ancient sites, such as the temple at Philae. Without rescue work, temples such as this may be lost forever. So if you plan to go on to become professional Egyptologists when you grow up, I will give you every encouragement!

Your Loving Aunt,

Emily

*Without a serious effort, the Temple of Isis at Philae, now partially underwater, could be lost to Egyptologists forever.*

THE ASWAN DAM

The Aswan Dam was completed in 1902 in order to control the regularly flooding waters of the Nile. It will help Egypt to develop and, it is hoped, become a country where drought and famine is a thing of the past.

PUBLISHER'S NOTE

We have reproduced Miss Emily Sands's journal much as it was discovered, so that it tends to reflect Egyptology as it was understood in 1926. However, there are a great many excellent modern books that will bring the reader up to date. One interesting fact is that the Temple of Isis at Philae, which Miss Sands refers to, was finally saved from the waters of the Nile when the Aswan High Dam was built – it was moved stone by stone onto a higher island nearby, as was the Temple at Abu Simbel, which also had to be reconstructed at a higher level.

8 March 2005

Dear Reader,

Emily Sands was not a trained Egyptologist, but she had read a lot about Ancient Egypt, met important scholars, and attended many lectures on Egyptian subjects. She clearly knew a great deal, but perhaps not quite as much as she thought she did. The fruits of her knowledge are in this book. If you have enjoyed it, and want to know more, even more than Emily Sands, or if you want to become an Egyptologist, then go as often as you can to museums that exhibit Egyptian antiquities, read some of the many useful books now available in good bookshops and libraries, and sometimes write essays about things you have seen and enjoyed. Even if you do not become a professional Egyptologist, you will always be able to enjoy Egypt and its wonderful antiquities.

With good luck and best wishes,

T.G.H. James

Formerly Keeper of Egyptian Antiquities at the British Museum